THE THUNDERBOLT

Heartthrob Hospital Book 1

LORI WILDE

D1521762

FROM THE MOMENT Dr. Bennett Sheridan stepped into the operating suite at Saint Madeleine's University Hospital, his freshly scrubbed hands held up in front of him and a tooth-paste-commercial grin breaking across his cover-model face, Lacy Calder was a grade-A, number-one goner.

She glanced up from where she stood perched on her step stool spreading autoclaved instruments across the sterile field, preparing for an upcoming coronary bypass surgery, when she turned her head and saw him standing inside the doorway.

Her heart gave a crazy bump against her chest, and her breath crawled from her lungs. Never in all her twenty-seven years had she experienced such an immediate reaction to anyone.

It was intense and undeniable.

Endorphins collided with adrenaline. Sex hormones twisted in her lower abdomen like a paint bucket in a shaker. Excitement, approval, and sheer joy sprinted through Lacy's nerve endings as fast as electrical impulses skipping along telephone lines, wiring urgent messages to her brain.

It's him! It's the Thunderbolt.

Oh, my goodness gracious, Great-Gramma Kahonachek was right. He wasn't some silly myth like Bigfoot or the Loch Ness Monster or the Tooth Fairy. Lacy was not the sort of woman who lusted diligently after complete strangers, and yet she was lusting after this one.

Big-time.

Step aside, McDreamy! Beat it, Doug Ross! Take a Hike, House! Move over, Dr. Dorian! Dr. Bennett Sheridan has arrived!

The man's Mr. Universe physique begged her to caress him with her eyes. He was tall, well over six feet, and broad-shouldered. He wore green hospital scrubs, but the normally shapeless garment seemed to actually enhance his amazing body.

With his arms curled upward, still damp from the mandatory fifteen-minute surgical scrub, she could see the hard ridges of his biceps bulging beneath thin cotton sleeves.

He possessed spiced peach skin as dark as an itinerant beachcomber's, and a firmly muscled neck spoke of time spent pursuing outdoor athletic activities. A tennis player, she decided, or maybe softball. His nose, crooked slightly to the right, announced that it had been broken sometime in the past, giving him a tough, no-nonsense air.

A fight, she wondered, or perhaps an accident?

His teeth, straight and white, flashed like a linen sail behind his widening smile. An accompanying dimple carved a beguiling hole into his right cheek. When his chocolate-kisses eyes met hers, Dr. Feel Good made it seem as if she were the only woman on the face of the earth.

Be still, my heart.

She felt an unmistakable "click," as if something very important had settled into place. Something that, until now, had been sorely out of kilter and she'd never known it.

At long last *it* had happened.

Lacy's knees turned to water. Her pulse hammered, and her tongue stuck to the roof of her mouth as surely as if plastered by creamy peanut butter.

"Morning, ladies," he greeted Lacy and the circulating nurse, Pam Marks. "I'm Dr. Bennett Sheridan, third-year resident on a study fellowship from Boston

General. I'll be interning with Dr. Laramie for the next six weeks."

They had known he was coming on board, of course. Dr. Laramie had made a point of bragging about the fine young doctor, summa cum laude from Harvard, who'd flown to Houston specifically to study under him.

A young doctor who'd beaten out three hundred other anxious applicants for the prestigious opportunity. What Lacy hadn't expected was that Dr. Sheridan would melt her heart with that let's-break-open-a-bottle-of-champagne smile or that she would experience the most desperate urge to razzle-dazzle him.

But how could she ever hope to impress a man so obviously out of her league? He was Mike Trout. She was the water girl.

His gaze landed on her and stuck.

A long, weighted moment passed.

Lacy gulped. Fully gowned and masked as she was, her hair covered with a sky-blue surgical cap and her feet slippered in matching shoe covers, Lacy couldn't help wondering why he stared so intently. Had she forgotten to put eye shadow on one eye? Did she have a smudge on her forehead? Was her mascara smeared?

Just her luck to meet the man of her dreams on the day she'd flubbed Makeup Application 101.

Unnerved, Lacy took a step backward and promptly somersaulted off her stool.

"ARE YOU ALL RIGHT?" WITHOUT EVEN THINKING about having broken scrub, Bennett Sheridan rushed to the fallen nurse's side.

Poor thing looked like a turtle flipped on its back. Her small legs were flailing wildly as she struggled to extract her toes from the hem of her scrub gown. Her scrub cap was knocked askew, revealing a hint of silky blond hair.

"Here," he soothed, kneeling beside her and placing one hand on her shoulder. "Let me help you." Reaching over, he tugged the corner of the gown from her foot. "There we go."

He looked down at her.

She peered up at him.

All he could see was a pair of soft, beguiling blue eyes the shimmering hue of lazy summer dreams peeking at him over the top of her scrub mask. Sumptuous eyes framed by impossibly long lashes that zeroed in on him with the precision of a laser beam.

LORI WILDE

Bennett blinked at the sudden sensation piercing his chest. He opened his mouth to speak, but no sound emerged.

"Do you hear music?" she murmured.

"Music?"

"Bells ringing, birds tweeting, angels singing?"

"Angels?"

"You know, those heavenly creatures with wings."

Thoroughly scientific Bennett cleared his throat, but damn if he didn't hear a faint refrain of *hallelujah* somewhere in the back of his brain.

"Did you hit your head?" he asked.

"I'm fine," she whispered.

"You've both broken scrub." The circulating nurse's voice cracked through the enchanting spell. "Get off the floor. Scrub in again." She clapped her hands. "Hurry. The patient is in holding, and Dr. Laramie will be here within minutes."

Bennett rose to his feet and held out his palm to the cupcake-size scrub nurse. She reached up and took his hand.

It was an extraterrestrial moment. An R-rated version of *ET.* Out-of-this-world woman touches man, generates ethereal glow, causes hot sparks deep inside his groin.

Very hot sparks.

Impossible.

6

He couldn't even see her entire face. This sensation had zilch to do with the young woman at his feet and everything to do with the fact he'd eaten a chocolate-chip muffin for breakfast. His blood sugar had crashed after the sugar rush.

Yeah, that was the ticket.

Not a testosterone overload. Not an endorphin rush. Bottoming out blood sugar. He needed protein. Good thing he kept beef jerky in his locker.

He tugged her off the floor.

She righted her cap and avoided his eyes. "Thank you," she whispered and started for the door.

"Wait," he said. "You've got something stuck on the back of your scrub pants."

"Where?" She turned her head and tried to peer behind her.

"Allow me."

Not knowing what demon possessed him, Bennett placed one hand at her hip to hold her steady. A soft, inviting hip that could easily have modeled gauzy, blink-and-they're-not-even-there undergarments.

He took his other hand and grabbed hold of the sticky red label plastered to her world-class tush and pulled.

Audibly, she sucked in her breath.

He was startled to discover she was trembling.

His heart stuttered, and he realized his blunder too late. He should not have touched her in such an intimate place. Not when he was having lascivious thoughts about that delightful bottom.

"Here you go." He cleared his throat and kept his voice neutral, belying the chaos rioting inside him. He placed the label in her hand.

It read: *Volatile, Handle with Care.*

Was that a message or what?

"Th-thank you," she stammered.

"Scrub in again. Both of you." The circulating nurse barked from across the room and pointed in the direction of the scrub sinks. "Now."

THEY STOOD SIDE BY SIDE AT THE DEEP STAINLESS-steel sinks in the scrub area, scouring first their fingers, then their hands, and lastly their arms with stiff-bristled plastic brushes and reddish-brown antiseptic solution.

Neither had spoken, but Lacy felt as if she was ready to explode.

Bennett began to whistle.

The sound pushed excited shivers under her skin. She cocked her head and listened, trying to identify the tune. When she did, she almost dropped her scrub brush.

"Hooked on a Feeling."

Was his whistling this particular old-fashioned song some kind of sign? Possibly a subliminal expression of his internal thoughts?

The Thunderbolt.

This had to be it. Nothing else explained her reaction to him.

Wait a minute, Lace. Hold your horses. For all you know this guy is married or engaged or gay or too wrapped up himself...

She glanced at his left-hand ring finger. Bare. But that didn't mean anything. Most surgeons didn't wear rings. Then again, the guy was a surgical resident, and few residents were married. Still, a naked ring finger was no guarantee.

Lacy couldn't believe fate would so cruelly lead her astray. Surely Cupid wouldn't send her a married man. Because that's exactly what this felt like. As if she had been shot straight through the heart with the winged cherub's love-dipped arrow.

Her friend down-to-earth friend CeeCee would call it "insta-crush lust" but Lacy knew this was different.

She recalled the feel of Bennett's hand at her hip, his fingers plucking the sticky label from her backside. An electrical thrill shot through her, tingling all the way to her toes.

Stunned, Lacy could not speak. How was it possible that the mystery man she'd been spinning elaborate fantasies about for half her life was poised a mere five inches away?

Since she was a young child, the women in her family had promised that one day she would meet her Mr. Right.

"But how will I know?" young Lacy had asked her mother.

"The thunderbolt," her mother had replied. "It strikes hard and fast. You'll just *know*."

"There's no mistaking it," her grandmother Nony had interjected.

"No point even looking around," Great-Gramma Kahonachek agreed. "If you don't feel the thunderbolt, then he isn't the one. If you do, then nothing can stand in the way of true love."

Growing up in a large extended family, listening to the romantic tales from the old country, Lacy admitted she secretly wished the thunderbolt was real and not a figment of the grandmothers' active imaginations. They had trained her to associate love with a strong physical and a fated mental jab that couldn't be mistaken.

The magic had worked for her mother and her

grandmother and her great-grandmother. If the thunderbolt theory was good enough for them, it was good enough for her. They'd all had long, and happy marriages and she wanted in.

Here at last was her thunderbolt in the flesh. With a mere smile, he had knocked her out with a clean one-two punch.

She accepted her emotions at face value. Dr. Sheridan was the man she'd been waiting a lifetime for. She knew it as surely as she knew her own name.

And yet, she was scared.

Terrified, in fact.

His sudden appearance in her world was a disruption of the status quo, and as much as she had longed to find her true-life partner, now that the time was upon her, she was afraid she would screw up her one chance at happily ever after.

Lacy experienced a breathless edginess, like a panicked swimmer dragged down by the ocean's hidden undertow. She wasn't sure what to do next. She couldn't very well say to him, "Hi, I'm the woman you're supposed to marry, and I wanna bear your children."

"What's your name?" he asked in a James Bond voice that caused a ripple of slick heat to roll down her back.

"My—my name?" she stammered.

"I don't want to have to shout, 'Hey, you,' every time I need a retractor."

His eyes twinkled mischievously, and his bold stare made her wonder if he had X-ray vision and could see past her outer clothing to her skimpy black lace matching bra-and-panty set beneath.

She had a thing for expensive underwear. Lingerie made her feel feminine, sexy, even when she wore baggy scrubs. She imagined his reaction if he knew what she had on right this very moment and ended up embarrassing herself.

Cheeks burning, Lacy swallowed hard and concentrated on scrubbing her fingers until they throbbed, desperate to sever her gaze from his.

Did he feel it too? This heat? This energy? This inexplicable *something*?

"Lacy," she finally whispered, frustrated by her shyness.

"I'm sorry, I didn't catch that." He tilted his head as if straining to hang on to her every word. "You have such a soft voice."

"I'm sorry."

"Nothing to apologize for." His smile widened and twin dimples appeared in his cheeks.

She knew it was dumb, but she had a really hard time talking to gorgeous men. Her tongue turned to oatmeal; her hand sprouted extra thumbs, and she stumbled and stuttered.

With the teenage bag boy at the grocery, no problem. Her middle-aged dentist with the bad toupee, no sweat. But give her a handsome, sexy guy, and Lacy morphed into the world's greatest klutz.

Maybe it was because she was the second of six kids, and she'd sort of gotten lost in the shuffle. She wasn't the kind to speak up for herself, although she knew she should.

Her friends told her she was too nice. Maybe that was true. Lacy only knew that it was difficult for her to make small talk. She worried about sounding foolish, and she figured it was better to keep her lips zipped and let people wonder than open her mouth and remove all doubt.

So here she was standing next to a mythological god in human form, and she could barely utter a single intelligent word. What good did it do to have found The One when she couldn't even speak to him?

"Lacy." She squared her shoulders and forced herself to speak louder, but she was still unable to meet his eyes. "Lacy Calder."

"Well, Lacy Calder, I'm charmed to make your acquaintance."

Charmed? Her?

Quickly, she glanced over to see if he was looking at her, but he was rinsing his elbows in the deep stainless-steel sink. Lacy took advantage of the moment and allowed her gaze to linger upon him, absorbing his essence, rejoicing in his overt masculinity.

He exuded strength and power. A woman would never be afraid if she had a man like Dr. Sheridan to protect her. Then, as if feeling her eyes upon him, he raised his head and boldly winked.

Ack! Busted.

Lacy blushed and dipped her chin to her chest. Thank God for her mask. It covered most of her face. The only things that could give away her errant thoughts were her eyes. As long as she didn't meet his gaze directly, she could get through this surgery.

Hurriedly, she kicked off the water with her knee then turned, hands up, and headed for the operating room.

She could feel Bennett's gaze burning her backside. Lacy gulped and hoofed it across the floor, willing her hips not to wiggle. She was concentrating so hard that she didn't even see the orderly pushing the supply cart.

"Lacy." Bennett called her name. "Look out."

His warning came too late. She turned but not quickly enough.

Wham!

The cart broadsided her. Supplies teetered. The orderly swore.

Lacy reached out a hand to keep the supplies from falling, but her sleeve caught on a shelf.

She jerked back.

Boxes began their slow slide to the floor. Catheters and instrument trays, specimen bottles and packages of syringes, an avalanche of equipment falling on her.

Lacy tried to leap out of the way, but her sleeve remained snagged. Before she could hit the ground, Bennett was there. His arms went around her waist, holding her steady and his breath seared warm against the nape of her neck.

Lacy flushed to her roots. He must think her the clumsiest woman in the entire universe.

"I've got you," he whispered.

And she thought wildly, inappropriately, *Yes, you do*.

❧ 2 ❧

AFTER THEY FINISHED their third scrub of the morning, they re-gowned and entered the operating suite at the same moment Dr. Laramie strode in.

Bennett started a conversation with his superior, effectively letting Lacy off the hot seat.

Mentally, she castigated herself for her oafishness. What was the matter with her? She had better get her head in the game. She couldn't be dropping instruments higgledy-piggledy during the surgery simply because the latest hospital heartthrob distracted her.

She returned to her stool and her instrument tray.

Not long afterward, the patient, a sixty-five-year-old retired construction worker who'd suffered a heart attack, arrived on a gurney, and their work began in earnest.

Lacy tried to focus on her job, handing Pam, the circulating nurse, the equipment she needed to prep the patient—antiseptic swabs, sterile towels, bags of saline. On automatic pilot, she moved through the activities she performed with experienced ease several times a day. Her mind restlessly toyed with thoughts of Dr. Sheridan.

Calm down, Lacy.

She couldn't afford to make rash assumptions. Too much was at stake. She needed to give her emotions a chance to cool off. Maybe this is only happening because her twenty-eight birthday was looming, and her biological clock is ticking.

It sounded good, anyway. Her rational mind tried to slacken the stampede racing through her stomach, but her heart wasn't buying one word of it.

He's the one, he's the one, he's the one. Her blood sang through her veins.

Helplessly, her eyes sought him again. She observed Bennett from behind as he spoke in low tones with the anesthesiologist, Dr. Grant Tennison.

She admired how the material of his scrub pants stretched across his backside. She noticed that the hair poking out from the back of his surgical cap and trailing a short distance down his neck was thick, wavy, and black.

More validation. Lacy had always pictured herself with a black-haired, brown-eyed man.

I want to curl up on the sofa and read the Sunday paper with him, she thought.

She wanted to roll over in bed every morning and find him snoozing on the pillow next to mine. She yearned to go to the supermarket with him and pick out favorite comfort foods together. She hungered to feed him ice chips from a spoon when he has a fever. She ached to learn how he brushed his teeth and put on his shoes and buttered his bread. She longed for him to ask her opinion—does this tie go with this suit? Or should he grow a mustache? She wanted him to worry when she wasn't home in time for dinner.

This man was everything she had ever wanted and so much more.

Drop dead good looks, stellar career ahead of him, a come-on-over-to-play-at-my-house smile, and most of all...

Fireworks.

Peering into his eyes had shown her a glimpse of what lay in store. An earth-rocking sensation she could not deny. Red-hot-chili-pepper sparks that took her breath and promised so much more.

Rapture skipped through her as she thought of

kissing him. How would it feel to have his full, firm lips snuggled flush against hers? His tongue eagerly exploring her mouth?

Bennett turned and gave her an I-know-what-you're-thinking-you-naughty-woman expression.

Swiftly, Lacy feigned intense interest in her work. She repositioned the instruments on the tray stand and breathed in stale air through her mask. The powerful lights beaming down on them seemed hotter than normal, stirring the flutters in her tummy.

Now that she had found him, how was she going to convince him that she was *his* Miss Right?

Her innate shyness had often hampered her in nursing school, and it was the main reason she worked in surgery. Here, she never dealt directly with the patients. She could help people without inter-acting with them too much.

It had taken her months to develop the working relationship she had with the surgeons and the other nurses. Her co-workers occasionally teased her about her introversion, but after six years, she had at last become comfortable in her job.

She must overcome this accursed shyness. She absolutely must. Otherwise Bennett Sheridan, aka the thunderbolt, would complete his residency at Saint Madeleine's and be on his way without anything

more having passed between them than a few mean-
ingful glances.

Lacy could not let Mr. Right march out of her
life. She had to do something to get his attention, had
to force herself to conquer her natural reticence with
the opposite sex.

But what?

And how?

❦

"GREAT-GRAMMA, IT'S ME, LACY."

"*Drahy*! Is that you?"

"Yes."

"You sound so far away."

"I'm on my cell phone at work." Lacy glanced over
her shoulder to make sure she was alone in the locker
room before speaking freely.

She had a few minutes between surgeries and
instead of taking a coffee break in the lounge, she'd
felt compelled to give her great-grandmother a quick
call. As if there was such a thing as a fast phone
conversation with her family.

"Oh, my dear girl, I'm so glad you called. I'm
missing you."

"I miss you, too."

"Have I got a story for you." Her great-grandmother's rich laughter rolled easily across the miles. "Frank Sinatra munched your cousin Edward's undershorts right off the clothesline. You should have Edward's face. Beet red!"

Frank Sinatra, whose eclectic diet consisted of everything from spray starch cans to potato vines, was Great-Gramma's favorite ram, named after her favorite singer. She raised a small herd of Tennessee fainting goats, who were known for their odd defense mechanism of fainting at the first sign of danger.

Except Old Blue Eyes' namesake was so ornery he rarely fainted anymore. Nothing seemed to scare him. Not even Great-Gramma chasing him with her marble rolling pin she used to make kalaches.

"Gramma, I don't have time to talk about Frank Sinatra. I've got something very important to tell you."

"What has happened?" Immediate concern tinged her great-grandmother's voice. "Something is wrong."

"Nothing is wrong." Lacy took a deep breath. She could almost see the tiny ninety-two-year-old woman hunched over the phone in the family's eight-hundred-square-foot kitchen in West, Texas. "Something is very right."

"Don't tell me...." She inhaled sharply.

"Yes." Lacy nodded. "It's happened."

Great-Gramma gasped. "The thunderbolt?"

"Uh-huh."

Her great-grandmother let out another laugh. "At long last. But wait, let me call to your mother and your grandmother Nony. They'll want to hear this, too."

"Gramma, I only have a few minutes."

But it was too late. Great-Gramma had already laid the phone down. Lacy heard the receiver clank against the antique oak kitchen table that had been passed down through five generations, and a wave of homesickness washed over her.

Just then the locker room door opened, and Pam sailed in.

"Don't forget, the next surgery starts in twenty minutes," the circulating nurse said before disappearing into the adjoining bathroom.

Rats.

Even with a closed door between them, Lacy was afraid Pam might overhear her rather private conversation. Pensively, she studied her locker. *Hmm.* She was small enough to fit.

Casting a glance over her shoulder to make sure no one else had come into the lounge, she opened her locker, wedged herself inside, and closed the door behind her. A spare lab jacket brushed against her face, and she had to balance on top of the street shoes she wore to work.

Inside the locker it was black as midnight and hot and stuffy. Just when she decided this was a dumb idea, her great-grandmother came back on the line.

"Now, drahy, we are all here. Tell us all about the thunderbolt."

"Hang on, Gramma." Lacy heard her mother's voice in the background. "Let me put her on speakerphone."

"These newfangled gadgets," Great-Gramma muttered.

"I can't talk long," Lacy reminded them. "I've got to get back to work."

"Sweetheart, this is your mama."

"And your Nony," Lacy's grandmother chimed in.

"Hi, everyone. I had to tell you I've been struck by the thunderbolt."

All the women on the other end of the phone rejoiced, laughing and telling her, "Congratulations!" Even long distance they were overwhelming.

As quickly as she could, Lacy filled them in on the details.

"So what's the problem, drahy?" Great-Gramma asked. "You got hit by the thunderbolt. That's all you need to know."

"I don't know how to approach him. You know how I get when I'm around men that I like. And this is ten times worse. I say stupid things. I fall down. I drop stuff. What can I do not to look like a fool?"

"You do nothing," Great-Gramma advised.

"He will come to you," Her grandmother Nony promised.

"Listen to your grandmothers. It will all work out," Lacy's mother said.

"But how can you be so sure?"

"Trust in the power of the thunderbolt!" all three chimed in unison. "It will never lead you astray."

"Okeydokey. Thanks so much. I love you guys."

"We love you, too," Grandmother Nony said.

"Bring your thunderbolt to see us soon," Great-Gramma said. "We want to meet him."

"Enjoy being in love," her mother said. "You deserve it, darling."

"Goodbye." Lacy severed the connection and leaned back in the locker, her heart pounding.

Love.

Was she really, truly in love at first sight? Maybe she was reading more into this feeling than she should. Maybe it was just sexual chemistry and not the thunderbolt at all.

That thought gave her serious pause.

She heard the locker room outer door close, and she figured Pam had left. Time to get back to work. Lacy pushed against the locker door.

It didn't open.

She fumbled in the darkness, her fingers grazing over the cool metal. No handle on this side of the door.

This was just ducky. She was going to be late for the next surgery. Pam would have her hide. Not to mention that she'd placed herself in a very embarrassing situation.

"Help," she said in a small voice. "Is there anybody out there?"

Silence.

She tried the door again without success. She would never live this down. She'd be the laughing-stock of the OR.

The outer door creaked on its hinges. She heard footsteps.

"Hello?" she tried again.

"Hello?" A deep male voice rumbled. "Am I having a conversation with a talking locker?"

"Uh, could you open the door for me? I sorta got locked in."

"Lacy?"

"Yes." Then, to her utter chagrin, she recognized the voice.

The door swung open, and she looked into Bennett's laughing eyes. He diplomatically hid his smirk behind a palm.

She wriggled her fingers at him. "Hi."

"Should I ask what you're doing in there? Or is it better if I don't know?"

"Just making a phone call." She stepped from the locker and held her head high as if it were perfectly normal to sequester yourself inside your locker.

"I've got a news flash for you, Supergirl," he teased. "That's not a phone booth."

She held up her cell phone as proof that she had indeed utilized the locker as a phone booth, but not before wishing the floor would crack open and swallow her up whole.

"Thanks for letting me out."

"Anytime."

"Well," she said, slipping her phone into the pocket of her lab coat and kicking her locker door closed with her foot. "I better get back to work."

"Ditto." He was still grinning.

Lacy inched toward the door.

"See you," she said.

"We're doing the same operation. I'm right behind you."

"Oh."

Feeling like a hundred shades of fool, Lacy turned tail and bolted down the hallway before she did something really stupid, like trip over her own shoelaces and go down in a heap at his feet.

3

"IT'S HOPELESS," Lacy moaned to her closest friends, CeeCee Adams and Janet Hunter.

"Hopeless?" CeeCee asked. "How?"

"Bennett's been at Saint Madeleine's for five weeks, and I haven't worked up enough courage to speak to him outside the operating suites. Not only that, but I'm sure he thinks I'm a complete idiot. And I could swear he's purposely been avoiding me."

It was late Friday afternoon, and the women were in Lacy's living room at the River Run apartment complex. CeeCee lived across the courtyard and Janet's apartment was directly above Lacy's.

River Run was a moderately priced development only three blocks from the hospital where they all worked.

Lacy had lived here for the six years since she'd

been out of nursing school, and until the past few months, she'd loved her little corner apartment with the great view of Washington Park. But lately she'd grown restless.

Suddenly, she had a desire for more space. A house to call her own. A front yard where she could plant flowers and grow vegetables. A place to raise a family.

Except she had no one to raise a family with, and unless she did something drastic to defeat her shyness, she might never get the opportunity.

She would spend the rest of her life in this tiny one-bedroom apartment, a lonely old lady who had missed out on her Mr. Right because she had been too paralyzed with fear to pursue him.

Try as she might to reassure herself that she was simply following the advice of the women in her family and letting the thunderbolt to take its course, in her heart, Lacy knew she'd embraced the path of least resistance.

Deep down inside she'd known all along that nothing was going to happen between her and Bennett unless she got brave enough to open her mouth and have a conversation with him. She had to make this happen. That's what was so scary.

"It's not hopeless." Janet reached for an apple from the fruit bowl on the coffee table.

Tall and willowy, with chin-length dark hair and inquisitive indigo eyes, she was Lacy's physical opposite. Janet had lived at River Run for less than a year.

Janet had recently completed her pediatric residency and was hoping to get in with the group of renowned pediatricians on Blanton Street whose offices were adjacent to the hospital.

"I'm proof of that." Janet smoothed imaginary wrinkles from her tailored gray slacks.

"What do you mean?" Lacy leaned forward. She and Janet sat on the sofa while CeeCee lay on the carpet doing crunches.

A physical therapist, CeeCee was fanatical about staying in shape. It paid off. In Lacy's opinion, red-haired CeeCee had a figure that could rival any movie star's and a sparkling personality to match.

"I used to be shyer than you," Janet told Lacy.

"Nobody's shyer than me."

Janet snorted. "Oh, yes. In med school, before I could work up the courage to go into my first patient's room, I had to stand in the hall and give myself a twenty-minute pep talk."

"It took me thirty minutes," Lacy confessed.

"See? If there's hope for me, there's hope for you."

"I would never have taken you for a shy person," Lacy said. "You're so self-assured."

"It's all an act. Or at least it was in the beginning.

LORI WILDE

Perceiving, behaving, becoming. If you believe you're competent and outgoing, then you'll become that way, and once you get over being shy, you'll never go back. Right, CeeCee?"

"Don't ask me." CeeCee huffed as she lifted her shoulders off the carpet and rolled forward. "I was born to socialize."

"I wish I could be like that," Lacy said wistfully. "I hate crowds and parties. It's tough thinking of things to say. I much prefer curling up with a good book any day of the week to the pressure of having to make small talk with strangers."

Lacy observed her friends. They brightened her life like fresh-cut flowers on the windowsill or home-made bread hot from the oven, slathered with butter, or soothing classical music on the stereo. She treasured them, and yet she envied them, too.

How she wished she could be more like breezy, fun-loving CeeCee or no-nonsense, down-to-earth Janet. Instead, she was a clumsy, meek wimp. Too shy to come out of her shell but hating her self-imposed isolation.

If it hadn't been for CeeCee stepping across the courtyard three years ago looking for a cup of alfalfa sprouts, Lacy would still be friendless in Houston.

It had also been CeeCee who, ten months before, had invited Janet to join them for a run in the park.

Since then the three of them had been inseparable. Currently, none of them had boyfriends. And until Lacy had met Bennett Sheridan, she'd been content with her life.

After she'd first laid eyes on him, she'd been unable to think of anything else. She'd confided her interest in Bennett to her friends but fearing their ridicule in her belief in love at first sight, she hadn't told them about the thunderbolt.

CeeCee believed that you made your own magic no matter what partner you were with, while cynical Janet didn't believe in romantic love at all.

"Lacy needs our help," Janet reminded CeeCee. "Got any great ideas?"

"Makeover!" CeeCee shouted gleefully.

"Makeover?" Anxiously, Lacy reached a hand up to pat her honey-blond hair, which hung in a single braid down her back, and she glanced at her loose-fitting cream-colored floral jumper. "What's wrong with the way I look?"

"No offense, sweetie." CeeCee drew her knees to her chin in a characteristic gesture. She was wearing black Lycra leggings, ballet slippers, and a stretchy pink crop top. Her tomato-red curls flowed like a flame across her shoulders, free and unfettered. "But you don't dress to attract the male species."

Lacy winced at her friend's honesty. True enough.

She purposely picked outfits that would not draw attention—no flamboyant colors, no short skirts or plunging necklines.

She preferred sensible clothing. Flats to high heels, stud earrings to dangly hoops, clear nail polish to scarlet. Yes, the more conservative her attire, the more secure she felt.

Except when it came to her undies. There she indulged herself, allowing her fantasies free rein. She could afford to splurge on panties, teddies, and bras. She had nothing to be afraid of. Men never saw her underwear.

"Why do I have to call attention to myself?" She frowned.

"Honey," CeeCee said in her quaint southern drawl, "why do you suppose flowers are so colorful?"

Lacy shrugged.

"To attract bees and butterflies."

"But," Lacy said, "I won't know what to say to a bee when he flits around my flower."

"You don't have to say anything," Janet told her. "You act cool, aloof, distant. Make them work for it."

"Nope," CeeCee argued, demonstrating the difference in their personal styles. "You smile and make eye contact."

"All right," Janet conceded, "but follow her advice

only if you're interested. Give the rest of them the cold shoulder."

"I don't want to impress anyone except Bennett."

CeeCee sent Janet a do-you-want-to-give-her-the-birds-and-bees-lecture-or-should-I look and shook her head. "The girl's got a lot to learn."

"What is it?" Lacy glanced at her friends. "Tell me."

"How did you get to be twenty-seven years old without picking up on some of this?" Janet asked.

"You guys know how old-fashioned my parents are. They didn't exactly tutor me on becoming a blond bombshell. Both my sisters are younger. On the rare occasions I had a date, my folks insisted one of my brothers go along as chaperone."

"And after high school?"

"It's always been hard for me to meet men," Lacy confessed.

"Things have got to change. If you want Dr. Sheridan to notice you, then you've got to get other men interested in you first. Guys are, by nature, commitment shy. You have to set the hook before you reel them in." CeeCee pantomimed casting with a fishing pole.

"I don't understand." Lacy moaned and covered her face with her hands. "This is too complicated."

"Come on, you can't hide out forever. Not if you want to win Dr. Sheridan's heart," Janet said gently.

"Yeah, get out there and have a blast." CeeCee nodded.

"Let me see if I understand you. In order to catch my dream man, I have to pretend to be a carefree party girl who flits from man to man without a concern in the world?"

"You've got it," CeeCee exclaimed. "That's the male psyche in a nutshell."

"But won't guys think I'm easy?"

"Yes, that's the whole point."

CeeCee's reasoning distressed Lacy. Couldn't Bennett just fall in love with her for herself? Why did she have to fake being a gregarious party-girl?

If he was only attracted to that facade, what would happen when Bennett discovered that she wasn't like that at all?

"What if I attract him and we start going out? What happens when he expects things to, er, progress further than a good-night kiss?"

CeeCee blinked in disbelief. "You mean you've never..."

Lacy shook her head. "Never and even if I wanted to go to bed with a man, I've got to be in love with him, and I want him to be in love with me, too."

"Hang on." CeeCee zipped from the room and

returned a moment later with a roll of condoms. She tossed it in Lacy's lap. "A girl's got to protect herself."

Lacy thrust the condoms at CeeCee. "I'm not ready for this."

"Keep it. You never know when it might come in handy."

Nervously, Lacy palmed the condom and dropped it into the pocket of her jumper. "I don't think I'm going to have to worry about a condom right this moment. I'm so shy. Let's start with that. How do I begin to overcome my bashfulness?"

CeeCee wrinkled her brow. "Can you think of a time you weren't shy?"

Lacy shook her head. "No."

"Wait a minute." Janet snapped her fingers. "Didn't you tell me you used to act in plays back in high school?"

"Yes."

"That takes guts. How were you able to overcome your shyness in order to get up on a stage in front of people?"

"Easy," Lacy said. "I was so busy playing a part I didn't have time to feel self-conscious."

It made sense. Acting had been her main social outlet in high school. She had enjoyed becoming someone else, forgetting herself, shedding her shell and emerging as the star. Could she actually do it in real life?

"How do we begin?" Lacy asked, excited yet hesitant. What was she letting herself in for?

"First, we give you a makeover."

"Then," Janet said, "we put you to the test."

"A nightclub." CeeCee snapped her fingers. "Where you can practice talking to men you don't care about before you move on to the good doctor"

"You two will come with me, won't you? I mean I don't think I can traipse into a bar on my own."

"Sure, we'll be there," Janet assured her.

"Thanks," Lacy said gratefully. "You guys are wonderful."

"What are we waiting for?" CeeCee asked. "Let's get going. The night is young, and the men are hot."

<hr>

"YOU'LL LOVE THIS PLACE," DR. GRANT TENNISON assured Bennett. They pulled into the parking lot of a noisy nightclub in the hospital district, aptly named the Recovery Room.

It was only seven thirty, but already the joint was packed. The thumping strains of heavy rock music jarred the walls of the large squat building decorated with flashing red-and-blue neon signs that simulated whirling ambulance lights.

Grant had offered to drive since Bennett was staying at the visiting physician's quarters at Saint Madeleine's and hadn't bothered to rent a car.

"Some of the best-looking women in Houston come here." Grant flung open the door of his late model Porsche and stepped into the muggy night air.

"Sounds great." Bennett was glad to be out of the high-stress hospital environment. He was going to have a couple of beers, relax, and enjoy the company. "It's been a busy five weeks. Laramie's a brilliant surgeon, but he's also a slave driver. I'm ready for a little R and R."

"I thought you had the air of a resident who'd spent too many long nights alone." Grant winked and nudged him in the ribs with his elbow. "Don't worry, you'll find what you're searching for in here."

Bennett certainly hoped Grant was right. He was looking for something to take his mind off Lacy Calder.

For some reason, Lacy absolutely fascinated him. Bennett had assisted Dr. Laramie with thirty-four cases, and Lacy had scrubbed in on twenty-eight of them.

Twenty-eight times in the past five weeks he had looked up to see those enticing astral-blue eyes across the table from him. And twenty-eight times he'd found himself aching to peel back that mask. Only once had he seen her without the paper covering over her face, and that was on his first day when she'd locked herself in her locker.

And each time he'd caught her eye, she quickly glanced away, but not quickly enough to hide the deep scarlet flush that rose to color the tops of her cheeks. Her shyness whetted his interest. If mere eye contact made her so flustered, what would a kiss do to her?

The idea excited him to the point where Bennett had to chide himself for the direction of his inappropriate thoughts. He had no business pursuing his co-worker, none whatsoever.

First of all, they worked together, and it would be stupid to allow anything to interfere with their professional relationship. Second, he was only going to be in Houston for another week. Not nearly enough time to get to know her. Third, even if they did click, he had another year left in his residency at Boston General.

Then he would be occupied setting up his private practice. But most important of all, he couldn't afford to be distracted during life-saving operations.

And then there was his personal credo—never, ever get sucked in by physical attraction. He was a man of science. He knew all about hormonal responses.

They had their place in the scheme of human reproduction, but rational-minded human beings didn't choose lifelong mates based on sexual attraction. He knew firsthand the chaos unrestrained chemistry could cause.

His parents had met, been wildly sexually attracted to each other, married a few weeks later, created a baby, and lived unhappily for two miserable years before calling it quits. Over the course of time, both his father and mother had reiterated their lesson, and Bennett, seeing their distress, had heeded their words.

Love at first sight was a myth. Lust, yes. Love, no. Never let your hormones rule your head. Make love to a woman if you will, but don't base a marriage on sex.

That was why he had dodged Lacy outside the surgical suite. He was afraid of the way she stirred his body. If he saw her go into the locker room, he avoided it for a while. If they passed in the corridor, he pretended he had something so important on his mind that he didn't notice her. If they ended up standing side by side at the scrub sinks, he always started a conversation with anyone else in the vicinity.

Although he felt like a heel giving her the cold shoulder, it was for their own good. He could not afford to fall in love, get married, and start a family for at least three more years.

He refused to go through what his parents had gone through. He wasn't doing that to his kids, nor to himself.

He had no time for a serious relationship, particularly a long-distance one. No, much better to enjoy the simple pleasure of working with Lacy and let it go at that.

Determinedly pushing aside all thoughts of the shy scrub nurse who'd so unexpectedly piqued his curiosity, Bennett followed Grant Tennison into the crowded, noisy nightclub.

Grant waded past a dozen closely packed tables near the door, making a beeline for the bar, calling out greetings to several people as he pushed past.

Glancing around the room, Bennett realized Grant had spoken the truth. The place was crawling with beautiful women. To the right of the bar was an archway leading to the dance floor where a disc jockey played a lively tune. Numerous dancers bumped and gyrated in time to the music. To the left lay a room that housed pool tables, pinball machines, and video games.

Leaning back, elbows against the counter, he

ordered a beer and studied the crowd. Bennett found people-watching fascinating.

When he was a boy, his paternal grandmother had loved to take him around with her because he could sit for hours in a shopping mall or an airport or a doctor's waiting room watching the crowds go by, wondering who they were, what their lives were like, where they were going.

Fond memories of time spent with Nanna were his most prized memories. It had devastated him when she'd died of a heart attack five years ago.

His interest in people, their motives and problems, was what had led him to become a physician, that and Nanna's absolute belief in him. He ached to be useful to mankind, to do something important and make his grandmother proud.

It was only later, while he was in med school, that he realized he loved surgery best and cardiac surgery most of all. What could be more fulfilling than learning the secrets of the human heart? By helping to correct heart disease, he was giving people a second chance at life, another opportunity to love. In Bennett's estimation, nothing was more rewarding.

He eyed the front door. Customers came and went. He recognized several people from the hospital.

Bennett was about to spin around on the stool

and ask the bartender for another beer when the door swung open and in marched three attractive women. Every head in the place turned to stare at them.

The redhead led the way. She bounced rather than walked. Her hair was shoulder length and curly. She was medium height with a body that wouldn't quit. A bubbly smile graced her lips, and she swung her head from side to side, greeting everyone in her wake.

Behind her came the brunette. Tall, slender, cucumber cool. She looked neither to the left nor the right but kept her head high and her gaze to the front. She had piercing ebony eyes and a no-nonsense countenance, and she wore an elegant black pantsuit, low-heeled black boots, and pearl jewelry.

But it was the petite blonde bringing up the rear that stole his breath.

"Will you look at her," Bennett whispered under his breath, his palm damp against the sweating long-necked beer bottle.

She moved with light, delicate steps, parting the air like water. Her hair, the color of moon drops threaded with gold, hung straight as a curtain down the middle of her back, and it was swept back off her forehead with a vibrant green bow. She was about five one, certainly no more than five two, and couldn't have weighed a hundred pounds soaking wet.

Her daintiness stirred his protective instincts. He had the sudden urge to scoop her into his arms and hold her safe from the rowdy crowd.

Her shoulders were squared, her chin up. She wore a barely there sheath of emerald green and matching four-inch stilettos. A gold choker glistened at her slender throat, and she carried a small gold clutch purse.

Bennett could not take his eyes from her.

The redhead scouted them a table and hustled her friends into place. The blonde took a seat with her back to him. She laughed at something the brunette said. It was a sweet, melodious sound.

A man in a cowboy hat came over to talk to them. He leaned down to whisper in the blonde's ear. She raised her neck. The action caused her pale hair to swish against her ivory cheek, and she tugged gently at her earlobe.

The gesture was so subtly seductive, Bennett had to give her credit. In nightclubs, most women were pretty obvious with their sexuality. Like the blonde's red-haired friend, but not this one. She exuded an elegant, old-world grace that took his breath away.

He wanted to know her.

No, *wanted* was too mild a word. He felt compelled to make her acquaintance. Something inexplicable was pushing him forward, urging him to get her phone number.

Wrapping his fingers around his beer bottle, Bennett got up and strolled around the bar, hoping to get a better glimpse of her face.

But before he could reach a vantage point across from their table, she took the cowboy's hand and allowed him to lead her to the dance floor. She cast a tentative glance over her shoulder, and her red-haired friend gave her an enthusiastic thumbs-up sign. Apparently, she approved the blonde's choice.

For some reason it bugged him that the blonde had selected the cowboy. If that's what she was looking for, then he was out of the running. Bennett was as far away from cowboy as one could get and still be standing on Texas soil.

Bennett went to stand in the archway leading to the dance floor. Several other men were holding up the wall, observing the dancers and waiting their turn to waltz with the ladies of their choice. Crossing his arms over his chest, he casually grasped the long-necked bottle between his thumb and index finger.

The disc jockey had put on a country and western tune Bennett didn't recognize. He watched while the cowboy two-stepped the blonde around the dance floor, her feet barely touching the ground. She was uncertain in her movements, as if she didn't two-step very often, but still graceful, nonetheless.

She reminded him of someone. Whom, he couldn't quite say. For no reason whatsoever he found himself wondering if her eyes were whirlpool blue.

Who was she? He had to know. As soon as the cowboy relinquished her, he'd find out.

Her hair swirled as she danced. Bennett found himself mesmerized, and he wasn't the only one. He caught many covetous glances angling her way from the men lined against the wall.

You're jealous, he thought, then immediately dismissed the idea. How could he be jealous of a woman he didn't even know?

What was this unpleasant squeezing he experienced deep in his gut as he watched the cowboy slowly slide his hand lower and lower until he was almost touching her firm buttocks encased so seductively in that snug-fitting dress?

The blonde didn't seem to mind that the cowboy was getting his fill. She didn't move his hand away or slap his face. She might enjoy being fondled in public. Had she come here intent on lassoing herself a cowboy for the night?

Bennett gritted his teeth and taste jealousy. This is completely irrational, Sheridan. Get over the woman.

Shaking his head, he turned away, unable to bear

another moment of watching the cowboy grope the soft flesh he yearned to nuzzle. It had been much too long since he'd had the pleasure of a woman's company if he was letting something like this upset him.

"How you doing, buddy?" Grant clamped a hand on his shoulder. "Having a good time?"

Bennett shrugged and wondered why he had come.

"I saw you eyeing that pretty little blonde. Very cute."

"You know her?" Bennett perked up.

"No, but she sure does catch the eye, doesn't she?"

"Yes," he agreed, disappointed that he wouldn't be able to wrangle an introduction from Grant. "How about her friends? Do you know them?" Bennett cocked his head toward the table where the brunette and redhead were surrounded by men.

"I know CeeCee, the redhead, everyone does."

CeeCee was very attractive, Bennett had to give her that, but in his estimation, she couldn't hold a candle to her fair-haired friend.

At that moment, the blonde returned from the dance floor—sans cowboy, Bennett was pleased to note. She passed right by where he and Grant stood. Bennett narrowed his eyes, desperate for a closer look. Her scent caught his nose as she floated off.

Roses. He'd smelled that perfume before.

Lacy?

His heart skipped a beat. Nah. Couldn't be. This vibrant young lady simply couldn't be the shy scrub nurse.

Then she stopped, turned, and met his gaze. There was no mistaking those Alps-blue eyes. He'd stared into them for hours at a time. Stared at those eyes and lusted after the woman who possessed them.

Coquettishly, she pursed her lips and blew him a kiss.

❧ 4 ❧

LACY FELT physically ill. Dancing with that cowboy and then blowing Bennett a kiss drained every ounce of courage she possessed. What had come over her? Hands trembling, she sat down at the table beside CeeCee and Janet.

Had Bennett recognized her? She had wanted him to, and yet the thought of holding a conversation with him caused her chest to squeeze so tightly it was a miracle she could breathe.

"You did great," CeeCee exclaimed, pounding Lacy approvingly on the back. "First time out of the hat and you dance with a guy! I'm so proud of you."

"He dragged me around the dance floor," Lacy muttered. "I don't really call that dancing."

"Jake's a nice guy, though, don't you think?"

CeeCee glanced over her shoulder at the cowboy. "He was a good friend to help ease you over your first dance and break the ice."

Jake the cowboy might be good friends with CeeCee, but he had let his hands do a little more roving than necessary. Lacy, of course, hadn't had the courage to tell him to keep his hands to himself, so she'd suffered in silence.

Lacy sighed. It was this ridiculous eye-popping dress and these silly three-inch spike heels CeeCee had forced her to wear that caused the problem. In her scrubs, the cowboy wouldn't have glanced at her twice, much less tried anything.

"Are you all right?" Janet asked. "You're pale as a sheet, and you're perspiring." She placed two fingers on Lacy's wrist. "Goodness, you're tachycardic, too, and your pulse is thready."

"I think I'm going to be sick," Lacy confessed, remembering what she'd done.

"Put your head between your legs, take a few deep breaths. You're going to be okay," Janet said firmly. "It's just an attack of nerves."

"I'll get you a glass of water," CeeCee volunteered and sprang up from the table.

Janet laid a comforting hand on Lacy's shoulder. "CeeCee doesn't get it, but I know how hard this is for you. Hang in there. I promise flirting gets easier the more you do it."

"He's here," Lacy whispered, ducking under the table and tucking her head between her legs. She studied the cement floor and noticed a piece of broken pretzel wedged in a crack and focused on it. She took several deep, cleansing breaths.

"Who's here?" Janet asked.

"Dr. Sheridan."

"Where?"

"Over near the restrooms."

"Which one is he?"

"Tall. Black hair. Great build."

"Nice tan?"

"Uh-huh."

"Oh, my, Lacy, he is gorgeous." She heard the approval in Janet's voice. "He's definitely worth overcoming shyness for."

Lacy closed her eyes. The nausea wasn't getting any better. "I blew him a kiss."

"What?" Janet asked in disbelief. She lowered her head beneath the table and peered at Lacy. "You've got to be kidding."

"No," Lacy said miserably. "That's why I feel so shaky inside. I can't believe I did it."

"Well, that's great. CeeCee's right. You *have* made a lot of progress tonight."

"It was a stupid thing to do. He's going to think I'm some sort of hussy."

"He will not. And even if he does, that's the point. But tell me, how did you work up the courage to blow him a kiss when you can't even speak to him at work?"

"I don't know," Lacy wailed. "You guys had me all gussied up in this sexy outfit, and I guzzled that wine."

"You had half a glass," Janet told her.

"I took your advice and pretended I was a sexy actress. I don't know what came over me. It's as if I was standing outside my body watching someone else inside my skin. I stopped, turned, and blew him a kiss." She covered her face with her hands and groaned.

"It's not the end of the world, sweetie. What's the worst that can happen? He doesn't ask you out."

But he has to ask me out, Lacy thought desperately. He's the one I'm going to marry! I felt the thunderbolt.

Suddenly, a pair of men's shoes appeared under the corner of the table. Shoes that were presumably attached to a man.

"Did you drop something, Lacy?"

Bennett Sheridan's voice made her cringe. Lacy wished she could curl into a tiny dust ball and blow away. What to do?

Lacy's innate fear warred with her desire to get to know him better.

Janet was no help whatsoever. "I'm off to the ladies' room," she announced.

No, Lacy wanted to cry out, *you can't leave me.*

"Take my chair, Dr. Sheridan," Janet offered.

Janet stood up. Bennett sat.

You can do this, you can do this, you can do this, Lacy affirmed, then raised her head and peeked over the edge of the table to find him studying her with a bemused expression.

"Beach babe, she thought. Pretend you're a gorgeous beach bunny. Sexy, breezy, without a care in the world, you're irresistible to men. You wear toe rings and tattoos and string bikinis. Think sexy, Lacy.

Sitting up straight, she painted a smile on her face.

"Do you come here often?" he asked, amusement in his voice. His eyes twinkled, and he folded his hands on the table, as composed as a philosopher.

"Fairly frequently," Lacy lied, surprised at her brazenness. Where was all this courage springing from? "I have a few other places I hang out at, too."

"Hmm."

"Hmm?"

"I hadn't pegged you for a party girl."

"Oh sure." She waved a hand. "I go out every night. Party, party, party."

He looked surprised. "I've been wanting to ask you out, but I figured you weren't the type of woman who went in for temporary hookups."

I'm not that type of woman, Lacy longed to say, but instead she kept her mouth shut and waited for Bennett to continue. In fact, she'd never had a hookup and at twenty-seven, her virginity had become her secret shame.

"Since I've only got a week left in Houston, I don't want to start something serious that I can't finish. But I certainly would enjoy showing a beautiful lady a good time. Especially a lady who knows all the hot spots in town."

"You would?"

"Sure."

His brown eyes met hers and Lacy gulped. The thunderbolt galloped through her, quick and hot. Her great-grandmother was right. There was no mistaking the sensation. It was at once electrifying and calming, stimulating and peaceful, passionate and serene.

So bizarre and unlike anything she'd ever felt before.

Bennett looked awfully delicious in his crisp white cotton shirt, starched blue jeans, and casual penuche-colored loafers. This was the first time she'd seen him in casual clothing, Lacy realized, and he did not disappoint.

"Are you asking me out, Dr. Sheridan?" Her heart did a free fall right into her stomach.

"Would you say yes if I did?"

"For fun only?"

"That's right." He cocked an elbow against the back of his chair.

"Nothing that would monkey with our jobs?"

"Absolutely."

"No strings attached?"

"None at all."

Damn it. Why wouldn't he stop staring into her eyes? Lacy felt as if she were falling, falling, falling into the abyss of his soul. Flustered, she peered at her hands and fought the heat rising to her cheeks. She was in trouble here.

Bennett leaned forward. He was so close she had only to reach out her fingers an inch or two and she could touch his tanned skin.

"You're not looking for entanglements, are you, Lacy?"

What was it CeeCee had told her? That all men were nervous about commitment. That they shied away if a woman acted too interested, too eager, too anxious to have a man in her life. The male of the species wanted a challenge, a competition, a prize.

"Me?" Lacy placed a hand on her chest and forced a laugh. "Want a commitment? Whatever gave you that idea?"

"I don't know. In the operating room you strike me as rather old-fashioned. Not that there is anything wrong with that at all."

"And what gave you that impression?" Lacy was amazed at the ease with which she spoke to Bennett, but this was important.

He was *the one,* and she'd do whatever it took to convince him of that. Even if it meant pretending that she wasn't particularly interested. The logic was perverse, but CeeCee knew what she was talking about. Men battled for the honor of dating her red-haired friend.

"It's the way you blush every time I look at you. The way you can't hold my gaze for long. Like right now."

What the hell? In for a penny, in for a pound. She picked up her half-filled wineglass, downed the contents, then swung her gaze to smack head on into Bennett's.

It took everything she could muster not to cough and sputter. The tepid liquid burned her throat, and she tried not to blink. She had to maintain eye contact to convince him she was wild and bold, not shy and tame.

He stared at her.

She stared right back.

The room seemed inordinately warm and humid, steamy almost, and the music was too loud. They were stuck in motionless observation.

Glued.

His eyes peered deeper and deeper. He was inspecting her, scavenging her face for clues to her emotions.

He did not want to get involved in a long-term relationship. He was looking for something casual, light. He'd made himself perfectly clear. To pretend she wanted the same thing was folly, and yet, if she did not, he would not ask her out. She harbored no doubts about that.

Getting him to date her was the key. Once they went out, once Bennett got to know her, then he would learn that he could not live without her. He would move to Houston and finish his residency here. He would discover there were no obstacles to their love.

According to the women in her family, the thunderbolt was never wrong. Going out with him on the pretext that she was expecting nothing more than a good time couldn't backfire.

This would work.

Then something horrifying occurred to her. What

if he was married and looking to cheat on his wife with her? Maybe he just wanted an out-of-town affair.

Lacy narrowed her eyes at him. "You're not married, are you?"

"Do you think I'd say yes if I was?" His eyes twinkled. "No, Lacy. I'm not married. I might be a lot of things, but I'm not a cheater."

She let out her breath. Thank heavens for that. But she had to act nonchalant, as if she wouldn't mind dating a married man because she was that disinterested in a long-term romance.

"Because it wouldn't matter to me if you were," she fibbed, and hoped the heavens would forgive her a few off-white lies. It was for a good cause, after all.

"Really?" He looked surprised for the third time that night.

"Yes."

"I would never have believed *that*. You're an enigma, Lacy Calder, sweet on the outside, naughty on the inside." He wagged his finger at her and grinned. "My grandmother used to say, 'Always watch out for the quiet ones, Bennett. They'll fool you every time.'"

"Your grandmother is very wise," Lacy said.

"Was. She passed away five years ago." A sadness came into his eyes then and the look touched her.

"Oh, I'm sorry. Were you close?"

"Very. She practically raised me."

"What happened to your parents?"

"Mom and Dad are both physicians. Their work usually came before changing diapers. Or their marriage, for that matter. They got divorced while they were still in med school. I was two at the time. They were going to put me in daycare, but Nanna had a fit and insisted she be allowed to take care of me instead."

"Do you have any brothers or sisters?"

"Only child. How about you?"

"I'm the second out of six. Two sisters, three brothers."

"Must have been fun growing up in a huge brood." Bennett sounded wistful.

"It had its moments." Lacy smiled, thinking of her boisterous childhood.

"Nanna was my best friend," he admitted, and that vulnerability touch her heart.

She liked hearing about his grandmother and how much he had loved her. It reaffirmed her belief in the rightness of her feelings for him. Bennett *was* the man of her dreams.

"Nanna sounds like a very special person." Lacy understood. She was very close to every one of her grandparents.

58

"She was." His soft smile was laced with more sadness.

Touch his hand, Lacy. Comfort him.

Her fingers ached to follow her brain's command, but did she have the guts? Mentally bracing herself, she reached out and covered his left hand with her right.

Mistake!

A big one.

Alarm bells went off. Fireworks, the likes of which she'd never experienced, shot through her. Suddenly all colors shone brighter; all sounds were magnified; all aromas smelled stronger.

Strobe lights flashed from the dance floor. The throbbing beat vibrated up through the floor. Voices buzzed around them. In the cramped room, she smelled beer and popcorn, cigarettes and aftershave.

He felt it, too.

She saw the flicker of response in his eyes. They were instantly forged. She to him. He to her. Cemented. Bound. Joined.

No escape.

This was absolutely crazy. Her breath flew from her body. All moisture evaporated from her mouth. Her skin tingled at the feel of his muscular hand beneath her own. Her heart leaped at his spicy, clean scent.

LORI WILDE

"I want you," he said, "very much."

He *wanted* her. She saw the desire in Bennett's handsome face and knew it was true. She shivered. All her life she'd hoped, yet feared, that she would one day be the target of such stark desire.

Lacy had ached for the thunderbolt to crash into her life, while at the same time dreading the inherent loss of control that accompanied it.

She couldn't take the pressure. Could not keep staring into those mesmerizing eyes. She dipped her head and sucked in air through her open mouth, desperate to get enough oxygen to clear her addled brain.

Lacy knew she should say something, respond to his bold declaration, but her shyness flooded back, more vicious than ever. She simply couldn't speak.

Trepidation welded her teeth shut. She wanted him, too. More than he would ever know. But if she told him that she accepted his proposal, if she agreed to his no-strings-attached proposition, could she surely change his mind? Was the thunderbolt really as infallible as her family insisted? Could she, after all, trust her emotions? Was she willing to proceed on blind faith when logic and common sense urged her not to be foolish?

"Lacy?" He murmured her name. He'd taken her

hand in his and was gently caressing her fingers with his thumb. "Did you hear what I said?"

"Uh-huh." That utterance was all she could manage.

"I want you so badly I can taste it, but I don't want you to get hurt. If this isn't what you want, Lacy, if you are looking for something special, no harm, no foul. We don't take this any further."

What to say? If she agreed to a frivolous fling, she could end up with a broken heart despite what her family said about the thunderbolt being a sure thing. What if this feeling she had for Bennett was not the thunderbolt at all but merely a severe case of lust?

If that were true, Lacy had never lusted after anyone before, not even a movie star. This *thing* she had for Bennett was mental as well as physical. At least two dozen times over the past five weeks, she had anticipated his every need in the operating suite, handing him instruments before he had even asked for them.

A rational-minded individual like Janet with a healthy skepticism for anything as fanciful as the thunderbolt might argue that Lacy was such a good scrub that she automatically knew what any physician would need under the circumstance.

But it was more than that.

In her mind, she could hear Bennett say "Kelly

clamp" or "Abbott retractor" before the words came from his mouth. Once he needed a rarely used tool, and she'd placed it in his hand before he'd even finished asking if she had one on her tray.

That's how closely attuned they were.

"I'd like to get to know you better," he said.

"Me, too. That is, er, you, I mean, not me," she stammered.

"Would you like to dance?" He gifted her with a gentle smile.

Things were moving way too fast. Flustered by the pressure of Bennett's hand on hers, disturbed by her vacillating emotions, and swamped by shyness, Lacy knew she had to get away from his distracting physical presence so she could think this through.

Frightened that she might say yes before she had time to consider the consequences, she pushed back her chair and got to her feet. The way she was going, if he asked her to shimmy out of her black lace panties, she would break her neck complying.

"Lacy?" A frown creased his handsome brow. "Are you all right?"

"Bathroom," she muttered.

A rowdy drunk winding his way through the tables bumped into the back of her chair. Lacy teetered on her absurdly high heels.

"'Scuse me," the drunk mumbled, then lost his balance and stumbled against her.

"Oh!" Lacy breathed.

She saw alarm on Bennett's face, then watched him push back his chair and lift his hands to catch her as she tumbled headlong into his waiting arms.

MOMENTUM drove Lacy's backside into Bennett's lap. Her legs flew into the air, exposing yards of creamy skin. Reflexively, he curled his arm around her waist, and cradled her body against his elbow.

"You're all right," he whispered.

The sexy feeling of his rock-hard thighs beneath her soft buttocks robbed her of speech. An acute throbbing sensation hummed straight up through her bottom, and unless Lacy was mistaken, she had raised an equally compelling reaction in him.

He wanted her.

Their gazes collided again.

She saw hot desire in his face—hungry, raw, dangerous. For her! Her excitement shoved into overdrive. Not even in her wildest sex fantasies had she imagined anything could be like this.

Don't blush, don't blush, don't blush.

How could she convince Bennett she was a free-wheeling party girl if her cheeks turned crimson at the slightest provocation? She had to prove that she was brash, brave, and bewitching. She could not risk retreating into her protective shell of shyness. Not unless she wanted to risk losing him forever.

Bennett had made it clear enough he wasn't interested in long-term commitment. Of course, he didn't know about the thunderbolt yet, but he would soon enough. Until the feeling caught him the way it had snared her, she had to convince him that she was anything but the marrying kind.

All Lacy needed was a toehold. Once Bennett opened up and gave her the opportunity, he couldn't help falling in love with her. Right?

It was fated. She was his destiny.

But what to do? How would an outrageous, adventuresome, no-strings-attached woman act? How could Lacy convince him that she was spontaneous, freewheeling, and took life as it came?

Kiss him, some impish voice in the back of her mind ordered. *Kiss him. Kiss him hard. Kiss him long. Leave no doubts about your intentions.*

It would be so easy. They were already pretty darned intimate with her body snuggled tightly against his and her right arm wrapped around his neck.

All she had to do was lean forward and gently run her tongue along his lips. Not that difficult, really, especially when she wanted to kiss him more than she wanted to breathe.

Lacy hesitated.

Bennett's respirations, she noted, were as erratic as her own, and he was still staring at her as if shocked that she'd tumbled headlong into his lap.

Kiss him. On the mouth. In front of everyone. That's what a sexually confident woman would do.

Lacy the sexually confident woman? The label felt unnatural and yet kissing him felt so right.

She was scared. If she were standing, her knees would be knocking in a deafening cacophony. Lacy could count the number of times she'd been kissed on one hand, and not once had she been the instigator.

Most of the kisses had been perfunctory good-night-after-a-date kisses. None of them had been mind-blowing. Truthfully, Lacy had never really *wanted* to kiss a man the way she wanted to kiss Bennett, but her natural reticence held her back.

Her shyness had always been a safety net, something she could count on when she got in over her head. Well, not anymore. The time had come to take control of her future. This was the man she'd waited her lifetime for.

No more stalling. No more fanciful daydreams. No more lonely nights. Not if she acted now. She had zero to lose and everything to gain. Might as well plunge right into deep water and see if she could float.

Tentatively, Lacy dampened her upper lip with the tip of her tongue.

Ready or not...

Bennett gave her a knowing smile.

Lacy knew there could be no halfway measures. If she kissed him, it had to be all or nothing. No half-hearted joining of their mouths would do. If she wanted to convince Bennett that she was indeed a woman seeking a casual liaison, then she had to act that way.

Lacy lowered her eyelashes and gave Bennett a come-to-me-big-boy glance from the corner of her eye.

His body tensed beneath hers, and his arms tightened around her waist. His gaze took on a hazy, hungry quality like a starving man offered a full plate at the king's banquet.

People were watching.

She felt the heat of their collective stares, and her skin prickled with awareness. Normally, Lacy would have been consumed by social anxiety at being the center of attention, but resting here in Bennett's lap, staring up into eyes as dark as midnight, she felt so wonderful that all self-recrimination vanished.

If the crowd was wishing for a show, then by golly she'd give them one.

Drawing in a deep breath for courage, she pursed her lips.

Bennett swallowed, his Adam's apple bobbing.

Anticipation. So sweet.

Later, thinking back on the moment, Lacy couldn't really say who kissed whom. She raised her chin. Bennett lowered his face, and their lips became one, melding into a blur of soft flesh—sizzling, powerful, electric.

Act the part. You're a femme fatale. A heartbreaker. A collector of men's affections. Give him all that you've got.

It was as if the entire universe was shoving her forward. An aching, urgent need she could not explain gripped her with primal lust. Amazed at her own boldness, Lacy poked out her tongue, urging his lips to part, to allow her entry.

Eagerly, he complied.

She slipped her tongue into the warm, moist recesses of his mouth, and she inhaled his sigh.

He smelled heavenly and tasted even better, a soothing mixture of poppy seeds, soap, and home-made bread. His flavor reminded Lacy of her great-grandmother's kitchen.

Great-Gramma Kahonachek had come to America from her native Czechoslovakia back before it was the Czech Republic. She canned her own pickles, baked her own yeast bread, and made her own soap.

Why Bennett Sheridan should smell like that unusual concoction, Lacy didn't know, but the aroma produced in her the warm, welcoming sensations of home.

Home.

Yes. She'd found home in his arms.

Greedily, Lacy drank from him. At last. At long last. Her fantasy man come to life.

Her eyes drifted closed as she rode the rising wave of euphoria. The sensation transported her far beyond the bar and into a place so magical she'd have sworn she was dreaming.

Bennett's mouth roved over hers, deepening the kiss. He hoisted her flush against his firm chest. Even through their clothing she could feel the rapid-fire pounding of his heart.

He was so strong, so virile. He made her feel as treasured as a five-year-old's favorite teddy bear.

Everything in her responded. Her nipples hardened. Her breathing quickened.

Blood rushed to the surface of her skin, bathing her in exquisite heat. An intense wave of longing crested deep inside her.

Lacy had never known it could be like this. This all-encompassing love, this crazy, cockeyed thrill, this incredible sense of rightness.

There was no doubt in her mind that Bennett Sheridan was her other half, her soul mate, her true love, even if he couldn't admit it yet. He was too caught up in his career, too worried about hurting her to take a chance on love, but Lacy knew better. She would use any means at her disposal to win him over, including pretending to be something she wasn't.

He would forgive her in the end. He had no choice. The thunderbolt had struck.

❧

BENNETT SHERIDAN WAS A GONER.

Kissing Lacy was like taking the express elevator straight to heaven. She lifted him up, gave his soul wings.

Adrenaline and testosterone shot through his system, propelling him to a level of arousal usually reserved for sex-starved teenage boys. He was flying, gliding on top of the world. Unfortunately, that only meant he faced a long downward plunge.

His head reeled. His gut clenched. His loins flamed. His heart hammered. And all for want of this wild little blonde thrashing madly about in his arms.

He had to break the kiss, had to get fresh air, had to do something before he ravished her right there on the table. Gasping, he wrenched his mouth from hers.

Applause broke out around them, and Bennett found himself blushing. He had never been so turned on in public.

Ever.

He prided himself on being a rational man, fully in control of himself and his actions, and yet in one brief moment, Lacy Calder had stripped him of his illusion. He was no better than a wild stag in the woods rutting for a willing doe.

His fingers were trembling. He jammed them through his hair and struggled desperately to correct the imbalance that knocked his world out of kilter.

Lacy was breathing hard, her chest rising and falling fast as a rabbit's, her cute backside resting in his lap.

Had she felt his arousal? Was she aware of exactly what she'd done to him? How could she not know? The evidence was as obvious as the nose on his face.

What an unpredictable woman! When he had first stepped into the operating suite at Saint Madeleine's and she'd barely mustered the courage to tell him her name, he had labeled her sweet, shy, and innocent.

A nice woman. The type of woman a guy took home to meet his mother. A happily-ever-after sort of woman.

A woman to avoid.

But Lacy Calder had fooled him.

Completely.

Apparently, she hid more behind that surgical mask than he could have guessed. Beneath that quiet, well-bred exterior lurked a lusty spirit.

Her kiss told him so.

The minute Lacy tumbled into his lap he'd known he was going to kiss her. He'd been fighting the urge for over a month.

And then their lips had met.

Bennett had been knocked down by the flood of her fervor. Her lips met his with an intensity that caught him off guard and kept him there.

Ravenously, he had embraced the delightful shock of her. Lacy had been the one to introduce tongues into the fray, not he, her warm moistness ambushing him, taking his breath.

Innocent? Not likely. This woman knew exactly what she wanted.

Him!

How could he have read her so wrongly? How had he mistaken this provocative siren for the timid girl next door? The paradox that was Lacy Calder both pleased and perplexed him.

Bennett wanted her as much as she wanted him, and yet something urged him to be cautious.

Be careful, tread lightly, don't lose your head. Or your heart. Remember, you promised Nanna you wouldn't marry until you'd completed your education.

But this was great, wasn't it? To discover that the woman who had so captivated him was not out-of-bounds after all? Learning that Lacy was not the marrying kind, that he could indeed act on these feelings she stirred inside him without fear of breaking her heart should have him ecstatic.

Instead, an odd wistfulness crept through him, and he couldn't say why.

He sneaked a peek at her. Her hair was sexily mussed, her lips sashay red and slightly swollen. Lips that brought back the delicious memories of his favorite childhood flavors. Cherry soda and cinnamon jawbreakers and strawberry Pixy Stix.

And those eyes, the soothing blue of Bavarian mist, drilled a hole straight through him.

She desired him.

No woman kissed a man she barely knew that

confidently unless she was prepared to take things to the next level.

But before he could accept the invitation her kiss offered, he had to be sure that was indeed what she really wanted. He refused to end up with a guilty conscience.

Having a great time in bed was all well and good, but it only worked if both partners knew the affair was strictly for fun.

Before he and Lacy took this relationship one step further, they needed to talk. But not in this noisy bar thronged nosy rubberneckers.

"Lacy," he said, "would you like to go someplace a little more private?"

6

SINCE THEY'D BOTH ridden to the nightclub with other people and neither had a car, Bennett offered to walk Lacy home via a detour along the river promenade as opposed to taking an Uber.

A full moon hung in the sky, illuminating the water in a silvery shimmer. This newly renovated area of the hospital district had the quaint feel of a European village. Street lamps lighted their way along a cobblestone path. Here and there, scattered footbridges arched across the river. Trendy shops, locked tight at nine p.m., sat bunched atop the retaining wall.

A slight breeze softly caressed their skin. From several yards away, they could still hear the vibrating bass emanating from the Recovery Room.

Lacy recognized the melody. An old Rod Stewart tune about a French girl losing her virginity. "Tonight's the Night."

Delicious shivers ran goose bumps over Lacy's arms.

"It's nice out here," Bennett commented.

"Uh-huh."

Since telling CeeCee and Janet that Bennett was going to walk her home and leaving the nightclub behind, her timidity had returned with a vengeance. Without the insulation of CeeCee and Janet, without the boisterous background noises as a buffer, Lacy felt vulnerable, exposed.

She wanted to be here. Oh, yes. Above anyplace else in the world, but she was unsure of herself as well. Too bad the thunderbolt didn't come with detailed instructions. She'd found herself alone with a man she'd only known five weeks but with whom she ached to become better acquainted.

Yet in an odd way, she *did* know him. In her heart. In her soul. If there was such a thing as past lives, then she and Bennett had been lovers in a previous one. Lacy had never felt such an instantaneous connection to another human being.

Her joy fizzed like uncorked champagne.

What should she say? What should she do? What did he expect from her?

But she needn't have worried. Conversation was unnecessary. So was action. Bennett took charge. He reached over and lightly enfolded her hand in his.

It felt so good. Her small hand enveloped in his large one. A perfect fit.

They ascended the walkway in silence, savoring each other's company. Crickets chirped. In the distance a dog barked. All anxiety vanished. All doubts evaporated. Peace and contentment stole over her.

"You're easy to be with." Bennett stopped beside a park bench beneath a streetlamp. Moths and June bugs flitted through the air. The scent of honeysuckle wafted over from a nearby fence.

"So are you."

"We work well together in surgery."

"Yes."

"It's like a dance."

"A tango."

"You feel it, too?"

She smiled like the Mona Lisa. She didn't mean to be coy. It was just her way.

"I can't help but wonder...." Bennett let his voice trail off.

"What?"

He pulled her close to him and ran a thumb along

her jawline. "What it would be like to make love to you."

Lacy sucked in her breath.

No man had ever spoken so boldly to her. If it had been anyone but Bennett, such a statement would have sent her scampering for cover, but he was entitled to say such things to her. He was her thunderbolt.

"Does that scare you?" His eyes glimmered in the moonlight.

Lacy shook her head.

"Because if that's not what you want, then say the word. We don't have to go any further with this...attraction. I know it's mutual. I see my own longing in your eyes."

"Yes," she whispered.

"I want you to know exactly how I feel. You're a beautiful, vibrant, sexy woman. I want to make love to you so badly that I can taste it. But I won't take advantage of you. I won't break your heart. I can offer you nothing but a week."

Fear raced through her. She peered up, searched his handsome face. His oaken eyes were serious. Bennett was an honest man.

Shouldn't she be honest with him in return and tell the truth? That she was already well on her way to falling head over heels in love with him? But if she did that, he would bolt. She knew it as surely as her name was Lacy Marie Calder.

"Are you willing, Lacy?" His breath warmed her cheek.

In answer, she brought his hand to her mouth and gently kissed his knuckles. His skin tasted slightly salty and the hairs on the back of his hand tickled her lips.

"Is that a yes?" Bennett asked, his voice husky with pent-up emotions.

"My apartment's only a few blocks farther," she said, terrified by her unexpected bravery.

Delight crinkled the corners of his eyes, and Lacy's stomach pitched.

What exactly was she letting herself in for?

They strolled along, still hand in hand, gazing at the stars, occasionally glancing at the river. She should have been happy and excited, but Lacy wasn't prepared. Could she really do this? Was she ready to make love to Bennett?

Her body cried *yes, yes, yes*, and her heart leaped with joy at the thought of their joining.

It was her brain, her common sense held her back. Even though she believed in the thunderbolt and trusted the guidance of her family, a tiny part of her nagged a warning.

Are you sure? Are you truly certain he's the one? There will be no going back. No undoing this once it's done.

"Those shoes look uncomfortable," Bennett said. "You're having trouble maneuvering in those things."

"Me? Oh, no. I wear them all the time," she fibbed, then instantly felt guilty for her additional lie.

"Wearing heels over an inch and a half is bad for your back," he said.

"I thought men liked women in high heels." And big hair and oodles of lipstick and eyeliner, at least that was what CeeCee kept telling her.

He slanted a sideways glance at her calves, and a speculative gleam came into his eyes. A gleam that made her shiver with delight.

"Well, the shoes certainly emphasize what nature gave you," he commented, "but there's no need to hobble yourself for the sake of either fashion or sex appeal."

She almost said, "I couldn't agree with you more." Instead, she simply nodded and took a deep breath.

"Why don't you take them off," he suggested.

"No." Despite the fact the shoes were chewing the skin off her toes, she shook her head. She would look too silly padding along bare footed beside him. He was already a good head taller than she. "I'm fine."

"Keep walking then?"

She nodded.

Bennett tucked his arm through hers, and they continued their stroll. Lacy concentrated on each step, cautiously placing her feet on solid ground. She didn't want to break her neck at this stage of the game. Not when she'd finally gotten him alone.

Except she had a major problem.

Now that she had him, what was she going to do with him?

Through lowered lashes, Lacy peeked surreptitiously at his profile that was cast in shadows, but she could still make out his regal nose, his firm jawline, his masculine lips.

She knew zip about seducing a man beyond what she'd seen on television shows or read online. Game playing was not in her nature, nor was manipulation. She longed for CeeCee and Janet's advice. They had gotten her into this mess. Where were they when she needed them.

Oh yeah, she'd left them at the bar.

The wind gusted and snatched at the bow in her hair.

She reached back a hand to hold the bow in place, but it slipped through her fingers and went skittering across the sidewalk.

"Oh, dear," she murmured anxious to put a little distance between herself and Bennett. Anything to give her time to think. "My great-gramma gave me that bow."

Forgetting about her precarious high heels, Lacy slipped her arm from Bennett's grasp and charged after her errant hair ribbon.

The bow blew off the sidewalk and tumbled toward the wooden railing separating the path from the river embankment.

It hung for a moment on a tall clump of grass. Just as she got close enough to reach for it, the wind gusted again, and the bow took off, taunting her.

Lacy lurched over the soft ground, damp from recent rains, determined to retrieve her bow before the wind sailed it into the river below.

"Lacy," Bennett called, "be careful."

But his warning came too late. The heel of her right shoe sank to the hilt. She jerked her leg forward in an attempt to extract herself.

The other heel stuck, too.

She stood with her legs three feet apart, barely able to stand.

She tottered to the right. Lacy windmilled her arms, tried to correct, and overcompensated. Her balance swung to the left.

The next thing she knew, she was falling forward. Her left foot had pulled free of the infernal high heels, but her right foot, oh, her poor right foot, was still strapped into the shoe, which was twisted at a very odd and uncomfortable angle.

She lay face down in the dirt, her bottom sticking in the air, dress hiked around her waist, her racy stockings and black lace Victoria's Secret panties clearly on display.

Ducky. Just ducky.

"Lacy," Bennett exclaimed. Immediately, he was on his knees beside her, his hands going to her foot, undoing the buckle at her ankle.

"I got the bow." She scrambled to pull her dress down and maneuver herself into a sitting position without putting any weight on her foot. She held up the wayward hair ribbon and tried her best to ignore the intense throbbing in her right ankle.

"I hope the bow was worth spraining your ankle over." Gently, Bennett manipulated her foot.

"Ow!"

"I'm sorry."

"How bad is it?" She struggled to peer over his arm, then gasped when she saw her ankle had already mushroomed to grapefruit size.

"Hard to tell. With luck, no worse than a second-degree sprain, but we need to get it iced and elevated, STAT."

"Oh, no," she moaned. "I won't be able to work."

"Surely you've got sick time available."

He didn't understand. She didn't care about missing work. What she cared about was missing him. He only had another week left in his rotation at Saint Madeleine's. If she wasn't able to go to work, she'd probably never see him again after tonight. Her bottom lip quivered at the very thought, and she feared she might burst into tears.

"It's okay to cry," Bennett said. "I know it hurts like the dickens. I sprained my knee skiing one Christmas."

The ankle pain she could handle. It was the other pain, the one deep in her heart, that made her want to cry. She couldn't let him slip through her fingers. If she had to, she would limp to work on crutches.

"Let's get you home." He slid one arm under her knees, the other around her back.

"Wait, my shoes."

He scraped the mud off CeeCee's high heels as best he could and handed them to Lacy. They were definitely worse for the wear. Then he bent, scooped her into his arms, and rose to his feet.

"Where to?" he asked.

"You can't carry me the whole way!" Lacy protested.

"Nonsense. You don't weigh much more than a hundred pounds."

"A hundred and seven," she corrected. "And my

apartment in the River Run complex is three blocks away. Just leave me here and go back to the Recovery Room and get my friends." She didn't want him to go, but neither did she want to give him a herniated disk.

"Don't be silly. I'm not about to leave you sitting out here alone in pain in the middle of the night." His tone brooked no argument.

My hero, my Prince Charming, my thunderbolt!

He held her close to his chest and started walking.

Her legs dangled over his bulging forearms. By this point, her ankle was pulsing with pain at every beat of her heart.

What a ninny. She had to be the klutziest woman on the face of the earth, but the wondrous effects of being held so close to the man she dreamed of outweighed the downside of a sprained ankle.

"I know you're hurting," Bennett said. "The best way to deal with that is to distract yourself. Close your eyes."

She peered at him.

He looked down and smiled. They had already covered half a block, and he wasn't even winded.

"Close 'em," he commanded.

She obeyed, letting her eyes drift shut.

"Okay," he soothed. The sound of his voice rumbled in his chest, lulling her. "I want you to think of your favorite place. A beach, a meadow, a mountain. Do you have a mental picture?"

Her favorite place? Why, right here in his arms. But yes, she'd play along. "Uh-huh."

"What do you see?" he asked.

See? Hmm, it was hard to visualize when there were so many distractions, the least of which was her sore ankle. Unable to visualize a picture of her own, she stole one from Great-Gramma Kahonachek.

"A meadow in the mountains with a babbling brook running through it." She recited by heart the description of Great-Gramma's girlhood home outside Prague.

"Very good," Bennett said.

What was very good was the heavenly way he smelled and the sound of his voice wrapping around her ears like the most lyrical of melodies.

"What time of day is it?" he crooned softly.

"Early afternoon."

"And the time of year?"

"Spring."

"Can you feel the sun on your skin? Can you smell the scent of lilies in the air? Can you hear cattle lowing in the field?"

Lacy tried to concentrate on the mental image, but what she felt were Bennett's arms holding her secure as steel cables. What she smelled was the fresh scent of starch on his crisp white shirt. What she heard was his guiding voice, distracting her from the pain in her ankle.

"Yes," she said. "I'm there."

"And we're here."

"Where?" She opened her eyes, and sure enough they were standing in front of her apartment complex.

"Which apartment?" he asked.

"Two seventeen."

"It *would* be on the second floor." He winced, but he certainly didn't look as if he'd just carried a one-hundred-and-seven-pound woman three blocks.

"You can put me down. I'm sure I can make it from here."

"No way."

"Please, Bennett, you've already done more than enough."

"Don't argue, Lacy." He started up the steps.

She thrilled at his forcefulness. Here was a man who took care of his lady. No doubt about it. He made her feel safe, protected.

"Keys?" He stopped outside her door.

She fished in the tiny purse and extracted her keys. She was startled to see her hand tremble. She'd never brought a man to her apartment before. Ever. Not that anything was going to happen between them now that she'd sprained her ankle. Lacy was both relieved and distressed at this.

He took the key from her and braced one knee against the doorframe. He juggled her against his leg to get one hand free to open the door.

A few seconds later, he swung the door inward, shifted her in his arms once more, and stepped over the threshold.

"Hang on," she said. "I'll get the light." Fumbling along the wall in the darkness, she found the switch and bathed the room in unexpectedly brilliant illumination.

They both blinked, then Bennett kicked the door closed with his heel, effectively shutting out the rest of the world.

"Would you like something to drink?" she asked. "Coffee, tea, soda? I'm afraid I don't have any beer."

"You're not up to playing hostess." He stepped across the room to settle her onto the sofa. "How about I brew you a cup of hot tea and then have a closer look at that ankle?"

"That sounds heavenly," she admitted. The only man who'd ever made tea for her was her father.

Bennett took CeeCee's shoes from her hands and tossed them in the corner. Then he plumped up two sofa pillows around her before peering at her ankle.

"The stockings have got to come off."

Lacy looked into his eyes. How was she going to get them off by herself? Yet how could she ask him to help?

He didn't even give her a chance to waffle. He leaned over and ran his hands up her leg.

She squirmed, giggled.

"Ticklish?" His grin made her insides quiver.

They were face-to-face, Lacy leaning back against the couch, Bennett bent over her, his hands under her skirt, fingers searching for the thigh band of her stockings.

"Good thing there's no one to walk in on us and misinterpret this situation," he said.

"Good thing," she repeated breathlessly.

What if her mother could see her now? Or her grandmother Nony, or her great-gramma Kahonachek. Would they be shocked at her behavior?

Or pleased?

Bennett's unintentional caress built a heated fire inside her. Lacy had to bite her bottom lip to keep from moaning her pleasure.

Oh! When would he finish this exquisite torture?

At last his fingers curled around the top of her stocking, and he inched it down, past her thighs, over her knees, then carefully eased it off her ankle. He repeated the process with the second stocking.

He rolled the stockings into tidy balls and dropped them on the floor beside CeeCee's shoes. Afterward, he took a third pillow and slid it under her right foot.

"Try to keep your ankle elevated. I'll bring an ice pack along with the tea. Although by the size of that ankle, we might already be too late to reduce the swelling. Do you have frozen veggies in your freezer?"

Lacy nodded, too overcome by the tender way he cared for her to even speak.

Don't take it personally, Lacy. He's a doctor. He's supposed to take care of people. That's what he does.

Bennett disappeared into her tiny kitchen, and she heard him opening cabinet doors, running water, turning on the microwave. She leaned back against the pillows, gritting her teeth against her aching ankle. Now that he wasn't coaching her through visualization techniques and his comforting presence was several feet away, the pain attacked with a vengeance.

"Do you take milk or sugar?" he asked.

"Plain is fine, thanks."

There came the sound of her sliding glass door opening.

"Hey," Bennett said, "you've got a balcony."

"Yes," she called. "It's what attracted me to this apartment."

"And you've got an herb garden out here. Rosemary, dill, thyme."

"How did you know what they are?" she asked, pleased and thrilled that he was so knowledgeable about plants. Lacy often dreamed of the day when she would have her own plot of land and could raise a real garden.

The microwave dinged, and a second later Bennett came into the room with a cup of hot water and a tea bag in one hand, a makeshift ice pack fashioned from frozen corn wrapped in a kitchen towel in the other hand.

"My grandmother," he replied in answer to her earlier question. "She had a green thumb. Some of the happiest days of my life were spent puttering in the garden with her. Of course she had me convinced I was the world's greatest weed puller."

"Aww. I love that image of you helping your gran in the garden."

He handed her the cup of hot water, then took a seat beside her on the sofa. Carefully, he applied the ice pack to her swollen ankle.

He looked downright boyish with that wide smile and his hair falling across his forehead. Lacy had a hankering to reach over and gently brush the errant lock aside. Instead, she focused on dunking the tea bag into the steaming water.

"I bet you *were* the world's greatest weed puller." She could see him now. Dark-haired and small, smiling at his grandmother, a handful of crabgrass clutched in his chubby palm. She caught her breath at the notion that someday she might have a miniature Bennett of her own, helping her in their garden.

"I smelled tomato plants when I was on the patio, but I didn't see them. Where are they?" he asked. "There's no mistaking that distinctive aroma."

"Along the outside rail." His interest in her garden tugged at her heartstrings. How could her feelings for him be wrong? A man who loved plants as much as she did? He *had* to be her thunderbolt.

"What kind of tomatoes?" He gently rotated her ankle. Lacy barely realized he was engaging her in conversation about the tomatoes so he could keep her mind occupied while he examined her ankle.

"Cherry and porter. My favorites."

"Mine, too."

"No kidding?"

"They're both so sweet." He paused, then added in a murmur, "just like you."

Their eyes met.

Oh, heavens, she thought. He's too wonderful. I'm going to ruin this somehow.

"When do you have the time to garden? I mean between nursing and your active night life."

Lacy gulped and shrugged. She wanted to tell him the truth. That she didn't go out often. That if it weren't for CeeCee and Janet, all her spare time would be spent either at the hospital or puttering around her apartment.

Instead, she said, "The plants don't take up much time."

"Still," he insisted. "Most of the driven career women I've known don't have much time for anything else. I haven't quite figured you out."

He thought she was driven? Hmm. Lacy didn't think of herself that way, but maybe she was. "What do you mean?"

He waved a hand at her skimpy dress. "You look like a sultry siren, and heaven knows you kiss like one, but you garden, and you're very polite, and you don't drink much. You've got an old-world charm missing in a lot of people now days. I like it."

"Those things aren't mutually exclusive."

"I know, it's just that..." An expression she couldn't decipher crossed his face.

"What?"

"Never mind." He got to his feet. "You're going to need an anti-inflammatory for the swelling, and you could probably do with a mild pain pill. I noticed there's an all-night drugstore next door to the hospital. I could go there, get you a prescription, and be back in thirty minutes. Will you be okay?"

"Fine. But you don't have to go to all that trouble. My friends should be home soon. They'll check in on me."

"It's no trouble, Lacy. None at all. I want to help."

What could a girl say to a gallant offer like that? Lacy smiled and nodded.

"Are you allergic to any medication?" He paused at the door to ask.

"No." She shook her head, distracted by the handsome figure he cut standing in the archway.

"Hang in there, kiddo." He smiled, and her heart swelled to capacity. "I'll be back in a flash."

He shut the door behind him, and Lacy let out a deep breath. At last she had Dr. Bennett Sheridan exactly where she wanted him, and all she'd had to do was sprain her ankle.

Who knew being a klutz had an advantage?

7

IN A DAZE, Bennett Sheridan wandered the
streets of Houston, his mind beguiled,
bewitched, bewildered.

He walked down the block, past an all-night
convenience store and gas station. He couldn't stop
thinking about Lacy and her smoking hot green
dress, and those make-love-to-me-big-boy shoes.

And that black lace underwear he had caught a
quick peek of when she had taken that tumble in the
grass beside the river. Who would have guessed she
was a racy lingerie aficionado?

And those stockings he'd had to remove. *Whew!*

At the memory, his body swamped with a sultry
heat. He recalled massaging his hands up her silky
thighs, peeling the stockings over her legs like he was
unwrapping expensive Swiss chocolates.

And the way she giggled. The sound had affected him like the effervescent giddiness of the finest French champagne.

She'd responded to his touch. There'd been no mistaking her languid movements, the ardent glimmer in her gaze, the deep, whispered intake of breath when his hands had briefly grazed her bottom.

Bennett groaned inwardly and fisted his palm against his forehead.

He wanted her too much.

No matter how hard he tried, he couldn't seem to consider anything but those innocent eyes blatantly contradicting that wickedly sexy kisses she'd plastered on his lips back at the bar.

She was as changeable as quicksilver. Shy one minute, strangely bold the next. He couldn't begin to explain her or his dangerously strong desire for her.

He remembered the feel of her in his arms, her soft derriere cuddled against his lap. He could still smell her scent on him. He held the sleeve of his shirt to his nose and inhaled deeply.

Roses, soap, and pure sensual woman.

Paradise.

But why Lacy? Why here? Why now, when his career aspirations prevented him from getting romantically involved with anyone long term?

What was it about her that so captivated him? This was not a good sign, not good at all.

It's been too long since you've had a woman, Bennett, old boy. That's all there is to it. End of story.

He did want her. He wanted her badly. But that wasn't the worst of it. What scared Bennett most of all was the way he longed to take care of her.

"Okay," he muttered under his breath. "Here's what you do. You get the pills, take them back to her, make sure she's set for the night, call her friends to come look in on her, then go the hell home. You've only got a week left in Houston. With that sprained ankle, Lacy won't be back to work for at least that long, and by then you'll be gone. You'll never have to see her again."

Why was that prospect so unattractive? He should feel relieved, not disappointed.

He wanted to be with Lacy, that's why. Wanted to be with her in every sense of the word.

But a woman like Lacy deserved a man who could give her unlimited attention and undying devotion.

"And you, my friend," he said softly, "are definitely not that man."

THE TELEPHONE JANGLED ONLY A FEW MINUTES after Bennett strode out the front door. Luckily, before he'd left, he had positioned the cordless telephone within easy reach.

It rang again.

CeeCee? Janet?

She glanced at the clock on the wall. Ten-thirty. Surely her friends hadn't come home this early on a Friday night.

She picked up the receiver.

"Drahy!"

"Great-Gramma, what are you doing up? It's way past your bedtime."

"*Pfft*. At my age there is no such thing as bedtime. You fall asleep when you're tried; you wake up when you're ready. Besides, Old Blue Eyes has the colic. He ate your father's bib overalls, metal snaps and all."

"Oh, I'm sorry to hear about Frank Sinatra."

"He'll be all right. What I'm worried about is you."

"Me?"

"Don't play coy, drahy. Five weeks ago you called me. Great-Gramma, you say, I've been hit by the thunderbolt. Then nothing. No call. No letter. You don't even email your mother. What's wrong?"

Lacy toyed with her braid. "Well, I don't think

Bennett's been struck by the thunderbolt. Can this thing be one-sided, Great-Gramma?"

"No. Absolutely not. He's holding back for some reason. When did you see him last?"

"Well..." Lacy began.

"Tell me everything."

It was easy to unburden herself to her understanding grandmother. She told her everything before adding, "It's hopeless. How can I make him fall in love with me when I can't even be near him?"

"You're saying he will be coming back to your apartment tonight?"

"Yes."

"Hmm," Great-Gramma commented, her voice changing in pitch. Lacy recognized that curious note. Great-Gramma was up to something.

"Hmm, what?"

"Just interesting to know. That's all."

"What are you planning?"

"Me? Planning? I don't know what you mean. I'm a little ninety-two-year-old lady. What can I plan?"

"I'm not falling for that," Lacy said. "You're as sly as a fox."

"Goodnight, drahy. Frank Sinatra is calling me."

And then the line went dead. Puzzled, Lacy stared at the phone for a moment before switching it off.

Ten minutes later two staccato knocks sounded on the front door.

"Come in," Lacy called from her position on the couch.

The door swung open, and Bennett stepped inside. Immediately, her eyes were drawn to his face like a magnet.

"Hi," he whispered, pushing a strand of hair from his forehead as he closed the door. "How are you feeling?"

"The ankle aches a bit."

Actually, it ached a lot, but she didn't want to be a crybaby. And, truth be told, the pain seemed to evaporate whenever he was near, her mind occupied with cataloging his virtues instead of dwelling on the ankle, which now resembled a lump of pasty yeast dough.

Bennett crossed the room carrying a white paper sack with an apothecary logo emblazoned on the side. He sat on the floor beside her and pulled two bottles from the bag.

"These should fix you right up. This one is to reduce the swelling, the other is for pain." He tried twisting the lid from the bottle of painkillers. It wouldn't budge. He smiled sheepishly. "Damn child-proof caps."

"Push down on the lid with your palm and turn at the same time," Lacy advised.

"Guess it's true what they say. Nurses know more about day-to-day patient care than doctors."

"Doctors have bigger problems than opening pill bottles." Lacy tried not to giggle as he continued to battle the stubborn cap.

"Blast it all," Bennett muttered a few minutes later when he still hadn't wrenched the wretched thing free.

"Would you like me to try?" Lacy reached out to lay a hand on his wrist.

"No, no. I'll subdue it."

The pressure of her hand on his must have flustered him—or at least she hoped that's what had happened—because the harder he struggled, the more stubbornly the plastic cap held.

Finally, exasperated but not ready to admit masculine defeat, he stuck the cap in his mouth.

He looked so completely incongruous, this serious-minded heart surgeon gnawing on a plastic prescription bottle, that Lacy began to laugh.

"You tink dis is funny?" he mouthed around the cap, sounding all the world like a movie mafioso with a mouthful of cannoli.

She nodded.

His eyes twinkled. He growled low in his throat and attacked the bottle with renewed vigor.

"If you jerk your teeth out," Lacy managed to wheeze between gales of laughter, "I won't be able to drive you to the dentist."

"At weast we got pwenty of pain pills," he replied.

"If we ever get the thing opened."

"I never gib up," he informed her.

Bottle cap planted firmly between his back teeth, Bennett gave a finally twist, and the bottle broke free.

"Yes," he gloated, removing the cap from his mouth and thrusting both hands over his head in a gesture of jubilant victory.

Men, Lacy thought with a bemused shake of her head.

Triumphantly, he doled out two pills. One from each bottle. A blue one for swelling, a white one for pain. He handed them to her.

"Fresh tea to wash these down with?"

"This is fine." She picked up her stone-cold tea from the coffee table and washed back the tablets.

BENNETT EYED HER.

Lacy was the cutest-looking thing he'd ever seen,

propped up on the couch. Too cute. Her sweet, incredible scent pushed him beyond distraction, and he couldn't stop staring at those creamy legs.

He should get out of here. Leave this minute. Instead, he found himself saying, "Maybe I should stay the night, just to make sure you're all right."

"That's really not necessary."

"What if you need to get up in the night? You might fall on your injured ankle and make the sprain worse."

She studied him a moment. "All right."

"Can I get you anything?" he asked. "Something to drink? A snack?"

"Well…"

"What?"

"I would like to get out of this dress and into my pj's."

"Your pajamas, right." He was talking lickety-split, and he knew it, but he couldn't seem to slow down. The thought of sliding a silky nightshirt over her head had him popping out in a cold sweat.

"Where are your clothes?"

"In the bedroom." She pointed down the hall. "In the bureau."

"Be right back." Bennett disappeared down the hall, wondering how he had gotten himself into this sticky-but-not-unpleasant situation and how he was going to get himself out again.

He flicked on the light in the small bedroom. This place reminded him of the Lacy he knew from the hospital. Old-fashioned. Shy. Sweet.

A queen-size bed sat in the middle of the room, adorned with a patchwork quilt. His Nanna had made quilts, and he recognized the pattern. Double wedding ring, it was called, or something like that.

Lacy's bedroom was impeccable. Nothing out of place. No dust or cobwebs or litter in the wicker wastepaper basket beside her computer desk.

Bennett stepped to the antique bureau in the corner. He pulled open the top drawer, dumbstruck by what he saw.

Panties. Dozens and dozens of panties. Thongs. G-strings. Garters. Scarlet lace. Black satin. Purple silk.

Drawn by an irresistible power, Bennett scooped up a handful and held them against his nose.

They smelled of laundry soap and rose-scented potpourri. He inhaled deeply.

The Lacy who owned these garments was not the Lacy he knew from the hospital. This was the Lacy who wore skimpy dresses and spike heels to go dancing with cowboys at the Recovery Room.

Then Bennett caught a glimpse of himself in her

mirror, a half dozen pairs of thong undies dangling from his hand, an I've-died-and-gone-to-lingerie-heaven expression on his face. Unnerved, he jammed the panties into the drawer and yanked open the second one, his breath coming in hard, short gasps.

All he could think about was Lacy wearing these delicate things.

He was dead meat.

SHE'D SENT HIM INTO HER BEDROOM. ALONE. TO rummage through her underwear drawer.

Lacy's face flamed. What had she been thinking? What if he opened the top drawer and saw all her sexy lingerie? What would be his impression of her?

The painkillers were starting to take effect. Not only had the pain in her ankle decreased measurably, but a giddy, light-headed feeling wrapped warm fuzzy fingers around her.

"Is this all right?" Bennett appeared in the doorway, holding a pink satin teddy edged with crimson lace.

Yikes!

The mere thought of lounging on the couch in front of him wearing that scanty number was more than she could fathom.

"Those aren't pajamas," she blurted.

His face fell. "Oh."

"But it'll do," she found herself saying for absolutely no other reason than to see him smile.

He crossed the room toward her.

Lacy's heart began to pound so loudly she heard her blood strumming through her ears.

He sat beside her on the couch, his body angled toward her head, his trousered leg resting against her hip. All her senses strummed with awareness while at the same time a heady warmth loosened her limbs and her tongue. She floated free, untethered, buoyed by pain pills and the giddiness of his nearness.

Her vision narrowed. She noticed everything about Dr. Bennett Sheridan, from the faint laugh lines etched into the corners of his eyes to the beard stubble gracing his manly jaw.

She also noticed that he looked uncertain and uncomfortable.

"Whaz wrong?" She giggled when she realized she'd slurred her words.

"The pain pills are making you a little punchy."

She nodded. It seemed her head bobbed on a string yanked by an invisible puppeteer. "Uh-huh."

Helplessly, he held her pink satin teddy in front of him. "How are we going to do this? Would you like me to leave you alone while you, um, get undressed?"

This time, she shook her head. "Gotta have help with this darned zipper."

"Oh. Okay." Still, he didn't move. He sat there with his eyes fixed on her mouth.

"You can touch me," she said, amazed at her own drug-induced audacity. "I won't bite."

Bennett leaned forward.

"At least not very hard."

HOW ON EARTH WAS HE GOING TO UNDRESS HER without driving them both wild with desire? The painkillers had taken over. The gleam in her eye was too bright, the way she looked at him too bold.

Keep her talking, Sheridan, he told himself, and whatever happens do not kiss her.

"If Dr. Laramie could see you now." Bennett shook his head. "He's under the impression that you're a sweet, old-fashioned girl."

Lacy lifted a finger to her lips, which looked especially soft and pliant. "Shh. We'll never tell."

He smiled. "No. It'll be our little secret."

"We've got a secret," she said in a singsong voice, then thrust her arms over her head. "Clothes off. Teddy on."

What had he done to get himself in such a

LORI WILDE

predicament?

Oh, yeah, he'd given her medicine for her sprained ankle, but his bungle had been leaving the nightclub with her in the first place. He was much too susceptible to her beguiling charms.

"Come on," she urged, leaning forward and twisting her torso so he could see the zipper behind her.

Hesitantly, Bennett reached out a hand and took the zipper between his thumb and forefinger.

Slowly, he inched the zipper down bit by bit, exposing the narrow expanse of Lacy's soft flesh beneath.

Heat swamped him. He bit the inside of his cheek to keep from groaning aloud.

Get yourself under control, Sheridan, pronto. Lacy's in a vulnerable state.

Gently, he tugged the dress over her head, his fingertips accidentally grazing her upper arm.

Lacy moaned softly and closed her eyes.

"Are you all right?"

"Perfect." She almost purred.

She was sitting on the couch, her legs propped on the pillow, wearing nothing but a black push-up bra and black lace undies. Her long apple-cider hair cascaded over her shoulders, descending to her waist like a golden curtain.

His fingers burned to touch her. His lips twitched to skate along her skin and taste the salt of her. His nose burned to burrow inside the fresh feminine fragrance of her cleavage.

Bennett swore he had died and zoomed straight to hell. Where else would he have such an exquisite creature at his fingertips and yet be unable to act on his very masculine desires for her?

His eyes ate her up, taking in the soft swell of her breasts, the luxurious curve of her hips.

Torture. Pure torture.

Cover her up. Quick.

Bennett stared at the tiny pink satin garment in his hand. As if it was going to do anything to cloak that magnificent body. Fervently, he wished for a floor-length flannel granny gown to toss over her.

Fumbling in his hurry, he threaded her arms through the teddy's spaghetti straps, then pulled it over her head.

She homed those breath-stealing eyes on him. "Thank you."

"You're welcome."

"I feel...kinda drunk." She rubbed her forehead with her fingers.

"It's okay. The feeling will pass."

Without warning, she reached up and wrapped her arms around his neck. "Kiss me," she whispered.

In an instant her lips were plastered against his. He wrapped his arms around her and held her close. His mouth came down with a fierceness that frightened yet thrilled him.

If anything, this kiss was even better than the one at the nightclub. Bennett dissolved like ice in a glass of hot water. He had no resistance to her. Whatever she wanted she could have.

Her hands roved over his body, gently exploring. She tasted of orange pekoe and smelled of rose petals. Her tongue teased, drawing him out, rousing myriad sensations inside him.

Her skin, her lips, her fingertips inflamed him. He tingled, burned, and ached.

Her breasts swelled against his chest. His pulse pounded in his groin as blood rushed to heat that area of his body. He reacted to her contact like a plant reaching for the sunlight. He awakened to the limitless possibilities of what could happen between them. Breathing heavily, he broke the kiss.

She grinned. "Hi, thunderbolt."

"Thunderbolt?"

Chucking him under the chin with a finger, she giggled. "Don't pretend you don't know."

"But I don't." What on earth was she talking about?

It's just the pain pills. Humor her until they wear off—

"Admit it," she whispered. "Admit you're my thunderbolt."

What the heck was thunderbolt? A horse? Anything to pacify her. "Okay, I admit it. I'm your thunderbolt."

"I knew it," she crowed and threw her arms around his neck. "Now take me to the bedroom and make love to me."

"Listen, Lacy." He cleared his throat and slowly disentangled himself from her arms. "Much as I would like to, we can't make love tonight."

"Why not?"

"You're under the influence of painkillers, and you don't know what you're saying."

"Yes, I do. I'm serious, Bennett."

He shifted away from her. "I won't be in town much longer, and while I think we would have had a great time together in bed, maybe your sprained ankle is a sign."

"A sign?"

"That a sexual relationship between us simply wasn't meant to be."

"I don't understand."

Oh, no. That sad, wide-eyed, lost-puppy look.

"I like you. A great deal. In fact, probably too much. Too much to make love to you and then just walk away."

❦ 8 ❦

THE ACHE in her ankle was nil compared to
the sudden stabbing in her tummy.

"Honestly, I'm a little old-fashioned," Bennett continued. "When I meet a girl I really like, and I know that there can't be a future with her, I prefer not to take the relationship to the next level."

What was he saying? If he liked her *less*, he'd be willing to make love to her?

"There doesn't have to be heartache," she insisted. No heartache at all. They could have sex, fall head over heels in love, get married, have a half dozen babies with his amazing dark eyes, and live happily ever after.

Oh, why had she let CeeCee talk her into pretending to be something she wasn't?

He reached out a hand and gently caressed her

cheek. "Don't get me wrong, cupcake. I want to make love to you so badly I can taste it, but I don't think it would be in either of our best interests."

"Bennett." She spoke his name because she didn't know what else to say. She had so much to tell him, but she didn't know how to begin to explain the thunderbolt to someone who hadn't grown up believing in its mythical powers, and she could barely keep her eyelids open.

And before she could form a coherent thought, Lacy fell asleep in the circle of his sheltering arms.

THE JANGLING PHONE JERKED HER AWAKE. SHE blinked, then realized she was snuggled tight against Bennett's chest. Lacy sat up straight, a little disoriented. What had happened? Then she remembered the pain pills and falling asleep in his arms.

Bennett yawned, stretched, and checked his watch. "Awfully late for someone to be calling. It's after one a.m."

"It's probably CeeCee or Janet checking to see if I made it home in one piece."

She reached over and picked up the phone. "Hello?"

"Lacy, it's Mama."

Immediately her heart sank. Mama never called after nine o'clock at night. Something must be wrong.

"What is it?" Lacy asked, instantly alert. She placed her palm on the arm of the sofa to brace herself.

"Honey, I've got some bad news."

She felt the color drain from her face and suddenly tasted her own fear. "What?"

"It's Great-Gramma Kahonachek."

Lacy's hands trembled uncontrollably, and she almost dropped the phone. "What's wrong?"

"We were up late tending to last-minute details for our booth at the farm exposition when your great-grandmother started having another spell with her heart like she did last spring. She's asking for you. Can you come home right away?"

"I'll be right there," Lacy said.

Instantly, her nurse's objectivity kicked in. The family needed her expertise. She switched off the phone and started to bring her feet up, but the pain in her ankle stopped her instantly.

"Something's wrong. You're pale as a ghost." Bennett took her hand. "And you're ice cold. What's happened?"

"It's my great-gramma. She's having chest pains."

"A heart attack?"

Lacy shook her head. "I don't know. She's ninety-two and she takes nitroglycerin tablets for angina. Bennett, she's asking for me."

The look of concern on his face was so touching that Lacy burst into tears. He gathered her to his chest and allowed her to sob. She soaked his shirt, but he didn't seem to care.

"I lo-love her so much," Lacy stammered when she was finally controlled enough to speak.

"I understand." He squeezed her hand and hugged her tighter. After what he'd told her about his grandmother, she knew that he did truly understand.

"I've got to go home. Right away."

"Where is home?"

"West, Texas."

"Where's that?"

"About three hours north."

"You can't drive." He shook his head. "Not with that ankle."

She worried her lip with her teeth. "The closest airport to West is in Waco, almost thirty miles away. I probably won't even be able to get a flight out before mid-morning."

"I'll drive you."

His offer touched her more deeply than she could express. "But I looked at the call sheet before I left work, and I thought you were on call for the transplant team in case a heart comes in for your patient, Mr. Marshall."

"I'm on backup call, and the chances of getting called in are slim. Besides, I can hop a plane back here if necessary. What is it? A thirty-minute flight?"

Lacy nodded.

"I'll call Laramie and tell him what's going on."

"If you're certain." She hated to put him to any trouble, but without him, she couldn't get to West before noon, and Great-Gramma needed her now.

"Consider me your personal chauffeur."

❧

THREE HOURS LATER, BENNETT GUIDED LACY's Toyota toward West, Texas. When Lacy told him that her great-grandmother was suffering chest pains, one thought held his mind—help Lacy get home as soon as possible.

He remembered his own nanna and how grief-stricken he'd been when she had died. The thought of what Lacy was going through prompted Bennett to drive her.

But the farther they traveled, the more he questioned the wisdom of his impulsive offer. Not that he minded going with Lacy. Not in the least.

The fact of the matter was, Bennett had a knack

for rallying in a crisis. His calm head in the face of adversity had earned him the nickname Dr. Cool at Boston General.

No, what bothered him was the instant closeness he felt to Lacy. Sharing a tragedy could create a special bond between two people. An unintentional sense of connection.

If he wasn't careful, he could get sucked into the emotionalism of the moment, and he might start believing the strange tugging in the general region of his heart had more to do with Lacy and not the situation at hand.

He had called Dr. Laramie and cleared his absence with the chief surgeon who'd taken him off the back up call list, but still, he would try his best to return to Houston if Mr. Marshall was fortunate enough to get a heart.

Outside, the moon had slipped behind a covering of clouds, leaving the highway bathed in darkness illuminated only by their headlights. At four thirty in the morning, there weren't many cars on the road. Bennett's window was cracked half an inch, and the earthy smell of fresh loam seeped inside the car.

As they'd driven, Lacy chattered anxiously, telling him that she'd been raised on a farm in West, a predominantly Czech community, and that most of her family still lived there.

Her grandfather, father, and brothers were farmers, she'd said. Her mother and sisters ran a general store in downtown West and her great-grandmother Kahonachek ruled the roost.

He sent a quick glance in Lacy's direction. His emotions were in a peculiar scramble. He felt confused, worried, and worst of all, desperately attached to this woman. She lay against the headrest, her hair spilling over the seat in a golden cascade.

Bennett's fingers itched to glide through those silken threads, and the urge to inhale the flowery fragrance of her hair overwhelmed him. Did she have any idea how beautiful she was? Did she possess a single clue how sharply his body responded to hers?

Before they had left her apartment, he had helped her pull a casual floral jumper the color of banana custard over the Cinderella-pink satin teddy. The playful outfit suited her much better than the racy dress she had worn to the Recovery Room, making her appear softer, more inviting, more fun.

He'd also wrapped her swollen ankle, cradling that delicate foot in the palm of his hand had almost been his undoing. He'd had the strangest urge to plant kisses all the way up that shapely leg to her thigh and beyond.

Now, every time he glanced over to check on that sexy little foot, he saw her cute toenails painted a provocative pink peeking over the bandage at him, reminding him of that moment in her apartment.

Her eyes were closed, but Bennett knew she wasn't asleep. Lacy rested, taking long, slow, deep breaths, fortifying herself for what lay ahead. Mesmerized, he watched the rise and fall of her well-rounded breasts, then realized his own breath was coming in short, ragged spurts.

Compelled to comfort her, Bennett reached over and gently patted Lacy's hand. The touch was like an electrical shock—intense, energized, startling. It was all he could do to keep from sucking in his breath.

Her eyes fluttered open. "Thank you for driving me," she murmured, her downy voice breaking the silence that had endured for the past several minutes.

"What are friends for?" he asked.

"Is that what we are?" Her tone teased, but the look in her eyes was serious. "I thought we were just co-workers."

Bennett didn't reply. They were just co-workers. They hadn't known each other long enough to become friends, although not seven hours ago he'd seriously been considering becoming her lover.

He was very glad they hadn't done anything more than kiss. Sexual relationships had a way of escalating in the flare of a crisis, even if neither party was looking to get deeply involved. The drama of sudden illness spotlighted the tenuous link between life and death and sometimes led to impulsive actions. At least, in his mind.

"You're certainly acting like a friend," Lacy added.

Friends. That was good, wasn't it? Far better to settle for friendship than to make love to her and leave in a week. Long distance relationships just didn't work. Been there, had the losses to prove it.

His common sense knew it was true, but his anatomy balked. His body wanted hers the way it carved water, food and oxygen. But sexual need and love were two very different things.

"How much farther?" he asked, hoping to distract himself.

"Almost there." Lacy sat up straighter and stared out the window. "Follow the main road until you come to the third traffic light. Then go three miles out of town. Our farm is on the right."

They would be arriving at the house soon, and he'd be meeting Lacy's family. Bennett winced at the full impact of what he'd gotten himself into. A total stranger amidst a close-knit group. What would her parents make of him and his relationship to their daughter? Did Lacy bring men home often? Were they accustomed to boyfriends popping in and out of her life?

Damn. This was going to be awkward.

When he had started out last evening with Grant Tennison, Bennett had wanted nothing more than to relax, have fun, and reduce stress.

How, then, had he ended up in rural Texas town, escorting a young woman he couldn't quite figure out? Lacy Calder was a paradox.

"This is it," she said.

Bennett turned down the graveled driveway leading to an apple-butter-yellow, two-story frame farmhouse with a big wraparound porch. A bevy of cars were scattered across the lawn. Lots of family had shown up for the emergency, he guessed. Pink fingers of dawn reddened the eastern horizon.

He pulled to a stop beside a weathered pickup truck stocked with farming supplies and Lacy unbuckled her seat belt and opened her door.

"Hang tight until I can get over there to help you."

He got out and from the corner of his eye noticed a clot of people forming on the front porch. Trying his best not to let the audience unnerve him, Bennett scurried to the passenger side.

"If you give me your arm, I think I can hobble up the steps," Lacy said.

"I'm carrying you," Bennett insisted. "I'm the doctor, so don't argue."

"Yes, sir." She grinned.

His heart lurched. What was it about her smile that affected him more strongly than the high of completing a successful heart operation? The notion that a woman's smile could be as fulfilling as his career was a new and startling concept.

Cautiously, he maneuvered her free of the car seat, hoisted her high against his chest, and started up the walkway to the house.

Amid cheers and applause, he stepped onto the porch, packed with what he could only assume were Lacy's numerous relatives. Over two dozen people were talking at once, flinging rapid-fire questions at them. Before he could put Lacy down, Bennett found himself introduced to brothers, father, mother, sisters, grandparents, cousins, aunts, uncles and neighbors.

The crowd ushered them into the house.

Dazed, Bennett merely nodded to everything. He, an only child, had never experienced the like. He remembered Nanna's deathbed vigil, with only him, his father and the medical staff in attendance. So different from this supportive gathering.

"Everyone, hold on," Lacy laughed, making the time-out sign with the fingertips of one hand pressed into the palm of the other hand. "Time-out. How's Great-Gramma?"

"She's in bed, resting," Lacy's mother answered.

She was a very attractive woman, no taller than Lacy, with short blond hair barely turning gray at the temples and a welcoming smile. She'd asked Bennett to call her Geneva and gently kissed his cheek. In another twenty years, Lacy would look like her.

"Wait, what? Why didn't you take her to the hospital?" Lacy demanded.

"She refused to go," said Great-Grandpa Kahonachek as he popped his suspenders with work-worn thumbs "She wanted us to go ahead with the farm expo. You know how stubborn my Katrina can be."

The whole clan bobbed their heads in agreement.

"She insisted she'd be fine as soon as Lacy got here," Geneva Calder said.

"I'll talk to her." Lacy nodded. "You can put me down now, Bennett."

"I'll take you in to see her," Bennett said, not terribly keen to be left alone with complete strangers. While they seemed friendly enough, they were eyeing him as if he was an exotic zoo animal.

Lacy must have sensed his uneasiness because she didn't argue, thank God.

"Okay. Up the stairs, down the first hall." She pointed to the stairway ahead.

Bennett carted her to her great-grandmother's room, careful to turn and step sideways down the hallway so as not to bump Lacy's ankle. Her head rested just below his chin and he could smell her sweet perfume.

For no good reason whatsoever, his chest tightened, thick with an unnamed emotion. He wasn't comfortable with this intimacy, and yet she felt so good in his arms, he never wanted to set her down.

He looked down at her.

Lacy stared up at him as if he were a gallant knight who'd slain a hundred dragons on her behalf. Her admiration both unnerved him and filled him with an odd sense of pride. No woman had ever looked at him in quite that way.

As if he was the most special person in the world.

What was he thinking? Bennett ripped his gaze from her face and stared at the door standing open a crack.

In unison, Bennett and Lacy peeked inside.

A bright-eyed elderly lady sat propped up in bed, a cat-that-chowed-down-on-Tweety-bird expression on her face. She looked quite healthy for someone suffering from an attack of acute angina and not unlike a queen holding court.

"Drahy," she exclaimed and motioned them forward. "Come in, come in."

"Drahy?" Bennett murmured under his breath.

"It means 'dear one' in Czech," Lacy whispered.

"She calls us all that, so she doesn't have to remember names."

"Good ploy considering the amount of progeny she's produced."

"Seven children, twenty-five grandchildren, forty-two great-grandchildren. But I'm her favorite."

"I can see why," he whispered, his breath fanning the teeny hairs around her ears.

Lacy turned her head and flashed him a smile.

"Don't stand there whispering. Bring your young man over here."

Bennett walked across the room and deposited Lacy on the edge of the bed beside her great-grandmother. This wizened matriarch had mistaken him for Lacy's boyfriend, but correcting her felt awkward, so he said nothing.

The elderly woman picked up a pair of glasses resting on the bed next to her and put them on. She eyed Bennett speculatively, then looked at Lacy.

"Yes," was all she said.

Lacy seemed to understand the code, for she nodded in return, then introduced him.

"Very nice to meet you," Great-Gramma said. "You're good to my Lacy, no?"

"Yes, ma'am." Bennett reverted to the old-school manners Nanna had taught him to use when addressing his elders.

Lacy reached out and took the elderly lady's hand in hers. "How are you, Great-Gramma?"

The woman pressed a dramatic hand to her chest. "Not so good at first, but I'm much better now."

"Why don't you let us take you to the hospital?" Lacy asked.

"No reason for a hospital. You're here. You can help me. You and your young man."

"Mrs. Kahonachek," Bennett said, "I'd advise you to seek professional advice."

"But you're a doctor, no? And Lacy is a nurse. That is professional."

"Well, yes, ma'am, but we don't have the equipment here to examine you properly or to make a correct diagnosis."

The woman's color was good, her respirations were even, and her droll smile mischievous. Bennett was beginning to suspect she'd experienced nothing worse than a bad case of indigestion. His own nanna had been known to exaggerate her symptoms when she wanted extra attention.

Still, with a heart patient one should never assume anything, and he wasn't doing to let down his guard.

"I'll get my medical kit from the car," he said. "And be right back to examine you."

"That would be good." She nodded.

"Be right back." Bennett hurried from the house, relieved that Lacy's great-grandmother appeared not to be seriously ill.

❧

"Oh, drahy." Great-Gramma squeezed Lacy's hand once Bennett had gone. "Your thunderbolt is so handsome."

"He is cute, isn't he?"

"I knew for sure if he drove you to see me if I was sick that he was the one."

"You're faking?"

Great-Gramma cocked her head and placed a palm over her heart. "Not faking...exaggerating."

"Great-Gramma! We drove three hours. He was on call and had to arrange for someone else to take his spot on the roster in case something happened."

"All for you." Great-Gramma gave a romantic sigh. "And he even carried you with your poor hurt ankle. What a hero!"

"Don't worry about my ankle. Tell me more about your chest pain. Even if you are exaggerating, at your age it could be serious."

Great-Gramma made a wry face. "If I tell you something, will you promise not to get mad?"

Lacy studied her great-grandmother's face, and a

sinking feeling hit the pit of her stomach. She narrowed her eyes. "What did you do?"

Great-Gramma looked to the door. "I'm not really having chest pains," she whispered. "I just need to burp."

"What? That's not exaggerating, that's lying!"

"Shh. A little white lie. Nobody knows but your grandmother Nony."

"But why would you fib?" Lacy laid a hand over her own heart. "You scared me to death."

"I'm sorry about that. It was a necessary lie. You told me the thunderbolt was going to walk out of your life forever and I couldn't very well let that happen, could I?"

"So you pretended to have chest pain?" Lacy sank her hands on her hips. "I'm not pleased with you right now.

"He won't leave you after this. You are in his blood, drahy. I can see it in his eyes."

"This isn't right, Great-Gramma, and you know it. If Bennett doesn't fall in love with me on his own, you can't force him."

"Pah. No one is forcing him to do anything. We're just getting him in position for the thunderbolt to smack him too."

Lacy stared at her great-grandmother in disbelief.

"For years you've been telling me that the thunderbolt cannot be denied. That it is infallible."

"It is."

"This doesn't sound infallible to me. In fact, this is beginning to feel more and more like unrequited love on my part and manipulation on your end."

"Oh, he loves you, too. I can see it in the way he looks at you."

"Then why do we have to play games?"

"Games? No games. You're dealing with a man, drahy. God bless their souls, they're often hard to convince, even when something is good for them. They are afraid to let go of their bachelorhood."

"I don't understand." Lacy was so upset she was on the verge of seeking out Bennett and telling him everything.

"All men need a little push now and then."

"But before you told me not to do anything, that our love would happen of its own accord. What about that?"

"And it will." Her great-grandmother patted her hand. "I just gave the thunderbolt a boost. Your great-grandpa Kahonachek, he didn't go down easy, either and your young man reminds me of him."

Lacy pulled back and stared at the wise old eyes peering at her. "So in other words, Great-Grandpa didn't fall in love with you at first sight."

Great-Gramma waved her hand. "Of course he did; he just had other plans, and he didn't want to change them. He was going to become a baseball player. Thought he was the next Babe Ruth." She chuckled at the memory. "But the thunderbolt can't be denied. He came around, and we got married when I turned eighteen. We've been happily married for seventy-five years on my next birthday."

"He gave up his dream for you?"

Great-Gramma sighed dreamily. "Now that's love, drahy. When a man decides you're more important to him than anything else in the world."

"What did you do to convince him?"

Great-Gramma smiled slyly. "We got lost in the Longhorn caverns together. Luckily, I happened to bring along a bottle of wine, a picnic basket full of his favorite sandwiches, and a soft blanket. By the time we found our way out of the caverns, he'd proposed to me and said I meant more to him than baseball."

"But what if he hadn't given up his dream? What if he had chosen baseball over you?"

"Then you wouldn't be here, would you?" Her great-grandmother reached up to brush a lock of hair from Lacy's forehead with dry wrinkled fingers. "Because after I'd been struck by the thunderbolt, I knew there was only one man for me. If not Kermit Kahonachek, then I would have remained a spinster."

"Really?"

She shrugged. "He is my soul mate."

"How can you be so sure?" Lacy asked.

"How can you not?"

"Because Bennett has a life of his own, a place of his own in Boston, he's his own person and I don't want to use tricks to make him fall for me."

"His place is with you. In Boston, in Texas, it makes no difference."

"You don't understand. Things are more complicated than that."

"You think things were easy for your grandmother Nony and Grandpa Jim? They lost a baby in 1948 and almost divorced over the sorrow. You think your mother and father didn't have problems? Raising six children isn't easy. The thunderbolt doesn't erase all difficulties, drahy. It simply tells you who you're supposed to spend the rest of your life with. It's up to you to make love last."

"That's not the story you've been telling me my whole life! You made it sound so easy, so magical."

"It is, if you don't try to complicate matters. There, drahy, don't cry." Great-Gramma handed her a tissue from a box resting on the headboard. "It'll all work out, I promise."

"Lacy?" Bennett stood in the doorway, the black medical bag in his hands. "Are you all right?"

She blew her nose. "Fine. Just a little emotional."

Simply looking at him, his hair falling boyishly over his forehead, that concerned expression on his face, tugged at her heart in inexplicable ways. Her entire body buckled. Her senses were so heightened that his long, lingering gaze brushed her like a caress. She felt as if she'd waltzed off a precipice into thin air, as if she were tumbling in weightless slow motion, spinning helplessly toward a shattering end.

Yes, she had fallen for him at first sight, but there was no guarantee he felt the same way. They'd been tricked into coming here by her great-grandmother's artless machinations and this felt more and more like a total disaster.

Bennett set the bag on the bed, opened it, and removed a stethoscope. Several of Lacy's family members appeared in the doorway, watching the proceedings.

"Hey, Lace." Her youngest brother, Jack, held up a pair of crutches. "Look what I found in the attic."

"Thanks," she said. Now Bennett wouldn't have to carry her everywhere. That thought both saddened and relieved her.

"I smell sausage," Great-Gramma said to Lacy as Bennett pressed the stethoscope to her chest. "Bring me some breakfast."

Lacy shot her great-grandmother a dirty look.

"Oh, no, you're having chest pains. You can't have sausage."

She wasn't going to let her great-grandmother get away with her meddlesome chest-pain stunt without paying some kind of price, but neither was she going to embarrass her great-grandmother—or herself—by giving away her secret.

But Lacy did have to get Bennett out of here as quickly as possible. Otherwise, the next thing she knew her family would be ordering flowers, sewing a wedding dress, and making an appointment with the preacher.

9

"SHOO!" Lacy's great-grandmother made shooing motions with her hands. "Everyone out of here but the doctor. You, too, Lacy."

"But Great-Gramma..." Lacy shot her relative a chiding expression.

"Go."

Bennett winked at Lacy. "Go ahead. We'll be all right."

"Are you sure?"

"Go have breakfast. I'll be there in a minute." Bennett figured Great-Gramma Kahonachek had something to tell him that she didn't want her family to hear.

He watched while Lacy hoisted herself up on the crutches, his eyes drawn to her petite body. How long had it been since he'd felt so helplessly overwhelmed by desire? He remembered all too well what it felt like to run his hands over her well-rounded body, to taste her lips with his tongue. His fingers tingled at the thought, as did other more southernly body parts.

"Close the door," Great-Gramma said, yanking Bennett from his fantasies.

"Yes, ma'am." He did as she asked.

"Now, go over to the bureau and open the jewelry box."

Bennett followed orders, humoring her. The heavy wooden jewelry box tinkled a melody when he opened the lid. He expected some Czechoslovakian tune, but to his surprise he recognized the music from an old disco song. Something about thunder and lightning and knocking on wood.

"Move those necklaces and rings aside. There's a false bottom. Lift that out," Lacy's great-grandmother instructed.

Curious, Bennett obeyed. He lifted up the bottom and found a pair of gold cuff links in the shape of lightning bolts. They were unique, unusual.

"I want you to have them," she said. "For coming this long way to check on me."

"Oh, no, ma'am." He turned to face her. "These cuff links look like a family heirloom."

"They're yours," she reiterated. "For taking such good care of my great-granddaughter."

Bennett shook his head. He felt very odd, and the cuff links lay strangely warm against his palm.

"Please, don't argue."

"I really appreciate the offer, Mrs. Kahonachek, but you don't have to pay me for being Lacy's friend."

"You're more than her friend, and you know it."

Her bold statement startled him. Bennett shifted his weight, uncertain how to extricate himself from this touchy situation. He liked the elderly lady. He liked Lacy's whole family. That was the problem. He couldn't have them thinking he was anything more to Lacy than a friend.

"Come, sit down." She patted the bed beside her. "Let me tell you about *my* thunderbolt."

Thunderbolt.

Wasn't that what Lacy had called him last night while she was oozy on painkillers? An edgy panic gripped him.

Great-Gramma reached out and folded his fingers over the cuff links resting in his palm. "Please."

Not knowing how to get out of it, Bennett cleared his throat and edged over, easing down up the bed.

Over the course of the next few minutes, Great-Gramma told him a wild story about how something she called the thunderbolt had struck her when she'd first met her husband and how she'd known from the moment she laid eyes on him that he was her true love. The cuff links, she told him, had been commissioned in honor of their love.

It was a touching, if somewhat batty, story. The exact opposite situation, it seemed, from what had happened to Bennett's parents. Love at first sight that lasted for a lifetime instead of ending in a bitter divorce. What a fanciful idea.

"Your family deserve these cuff links. I can't accept them."

"The thunderbolt cannot be denied. Take them," she whispered. "You *must*."

THE MORE SHE THOUGHT ABOUT HER GREAT-grandmother's deception, the more exasperated she became. Lacy, an honest person by nature, disliked subterfuge.

First, she'd allowed herself to be influenced by Janet and CeeCee's advice, dressing sexy, flirting, pretending she was something she wasn't, and now this. Great-Gramma was pulling the strings, and she expected both Lacy and Bennett to dance to her tune.

Thunderbolt, indeed.

It angered her to think that she'd spent her entire

adulthood waiting for the legendary whack of love at first sight. She'd even used the thunderbolt as an excuse to hide behind her shyness. She'd put her life on hold. She'd held her figurative breath and waited for the proverbial knight in shining armor to come swoop her up.

Lies. All lies.

To realize that all this time she could have been having fun, meeting fun men, coming out of her shell, learning and growing. Just as CeeCee and Janet had been trying to tell her. Yet she'd been too steeped in family tradition to take the chance.

But part of her clung to a belief that the thunderbolt was true. That she and Bennett were indeed meant to be together for a lifetime. Silly. Fanciful fable.

Lacy paced the hallway on her crutches. What was Great-Gramma telling him? She pressed her ear against the door and heard nothing but muted whispers.

Unable to stand not knowing what was going on inside that bedroom for one minute longer, Lacy knocked then pushed the door open. She saw Bennett sitting on the bed beside Great-Gramma.

Her gaze met his.

He winked at her, and her heart lurched.

They had to leave before things got really

awkward and since Great-Gramma was fitter than a Stradivarius, there was no time like the present.

"Since you're feeling better, Great-Gramma, I think Bennett and I will go back to Houston."

"What's your hurry, drahy? We don't get to see you often enough. Besides, you haven't had any sleep. See, your young man is yawning."

Indeed, Bennett was covering his mouth with his palm. He looked sheepish.

"Yes, but Bennett has a patient waiting for a heart transplant and he would like to be there if one comes in. It's better if we leave right away."

Great-Gramma laid a hand across her chest, leaned her head against the pillow, and closed her eyes. "Oh! My heart just gave a strange flutter."

In an instant, Bennett had his hand on her great-grandmother's wrist, checking her pulse, a look of concern in his dark eyes.

"It's not going to work," Lacy said. "We're leaving."

Great-Gramma opened one eye. "Fine. Scoot. Leave when I need you most."

"If you were really sick, you'd let us take you to the hospital." Lacy wasn't going to give in to her great-grandmother's maneuvers. Not this time. Enough was enough.

"Lacy," Bennett said. "Do you really think it's a good idea to agitate her?"

"Trust me. She's fine."

"Could I talk to you in the hall?" Bennett asked.

"Sure."

Once outside the room, Bennett lowered his voice to a whisper and leaned in close. "Listen, Lacy, I don't mind staying awhile longer to make sure your great-grandmother is all right. If you want to leave on account of me, don't even consider it a problem. Laramie said it's not vital that I be there if a heart should become available for Mr. Marshall."

"But would your first heart transplant with Dr. Laramie and that's why you came to Saint Madeleine's. To work with the best of the best. If you miss out on this, you'll kick yourself."

"First of all, the chances are slim that they'll find a match for Mr. Marshall this weekend, but if I do get a text, we can drive to the airport in Waco then fly to Houston. I can come back for your car later."

"That's really nice of you," she said. "But something tells me Great-Gramma is going to be just fine. We should leave now."

"You never can tell with a woman of her age."

"I already feel guilty enough forcing you to drive me here over a false alarm."

"You didn't force me to do anything, Lacy. I'm here because I want to be here."

Oh, Lord, he was saying all the right things. She looked into his eyes and melted. He was a good person. That didn't make him *her* perfect mate.

"Bennett, I think it's best if we return to Houston. That is, if you feel up to the driving without having had any sleep."

"Are you kidding? I've only been up twenty-four hours. That's nothing. When I was an intern, we worked thirty-six-hour shifts, and plenty of times we weren't able to grab a nap. I can manage."

Lacy nodded. "Then let's tell everyone goodbye and hit the road."

She hobbled inside the bedroom to inform Great-Gramma they were leaving.

"You've got your heart set on this?" Great-Gramma asked.

"I refuse to force anything between Bennett and me," Lacy told her.

"You're a stubborn one, drahy. You take after your old great-granny."

Lacy leaned over and kissed her forehead. "I love you, and I appreciate you trying to help. But I can't keep lying to him. If he wants me for me, fine. If not..." It took everything she could muster to shrug nonchalantly. "Such is life."

"Could you send your grandmother Nony in here before you go?"

"Sure."

Lacy bid her great-grandmother farewell and went to where Bennett waited. Together they went down to talk to the rest of the family seated around the breakfast table. Lacy gave Grandmother Nony Great-Gramma's message, then proceeded to tell everyone else goodbye.

"Stay and eat breakfast," her mother encouraged.

Lacy shook her head. It was too tempting to stay. Too tempting to eat and sleep and to allow her family to run her life. She'd been doing it for twenty-seven years. It was way past time to walk her own path.

"Bennett, talk some sense into her." Lacy's mother turned to him for help.

He raised his palms and laughed. "Hey, I'm only the chauffeur."

"We really gotta go, Mom," Lacy said. "I'm sure Great-Gramma is going to be fine. She probably had a bad case of indigestion. You guys have fun at the farm expo."

After many hugs and goodbyes, they finally broke away. On the way to the car, Bennett walked beside Lacy on her crutches, opened the passenger side door for her, then helped her slide inside.

Feeling wrung out and discouraged but with an

unexplained urgency pushing her toward Houston, Lacy leaned against the headrest and sighed deeply. She needed to get to her apartment, be by herself to sort out her tumultuous emotions.

Bennett got behind the wheel, and it took everything she had to keep from telling him to floor it. He attempted to start the car.

Dead silence.

He tried again.

Nothing.

He looked at her. "How old is your battery?"

"Bought it about six months ago."

"That's probably not it, then." Bennett stroked his jaw with a thumb and forefinger. "Unfortunately, I don't know much about cars."

She was about as lucky as a three-legged, one-eyed, bobbed-tail dog. She'd wanted nothing more than to escape the cloying bosom of her well-meaning but interfering family, and here she was stuck right in the middle of them.

Car trouble, of all things.

"Breakfast and a nap are beginning to look very appealing," Bennett said.

"Yes." Lacy sighed. Too appealing.

"Besides, if we stay a little longer, we can make sure your great-grandmother really is doing okay."

Lacy bit her tongue to keep from telling him that

sweet little old lady was lying like a politician and faking her chest pains. If Lacy told him that, then she'd have to reveal why.

"DYLAN CAN HAVE A LOOK AT YOUR CAR WHEN HE gets home from the expo. I'm sure it's nothing he can't handle," Geneva Calder told her daughter as she leaned between Bennett's and Lacy's chairs and raked a pile of fluffy scrambled eggs onto their plates.

Blue china plates. Wedgwood. Bennett knew because Nanna had once owned a set. Those blue china plates brought back a lot of fond memories.

He eyed the meal spread before them. Sausages and French toast, kolaches and buttermilk biscuits, hash browns and fresh fruit cut into bite-size chunks. There was a pitcher of milk, a carafe of orange juice, and a pot of fresh brewed coffee. He'd never seen a spread like this outside a hotel buffet line. His mouth watered, and his stomach grumbled. He was starving.

"But the expo won't be over until eight o'clock tonight," Lacy protested.

"By then you and Bennett will have had a lovely nap, and you'll be refreshed for your drive home."

Lacy sighed, and Bennett wondered, not for the first time, why she was so anxious to get back to

Houston. Granted, her great-grandmother seemed to be fine, but her family was so loving, so accepting, he couldn't figure out why she didn't want to spend more time with them. Hell, he would have given his right arm to have a close-knit family like this one and that was quite a sacrifice for a surgeon.

Lacy sat next to him, her crutches propped against the wall beside her. She kept casting surreptitious glances his way. If he were being honest with himself, he would admit to searching for her gaze time and time again.

Here, surrounded by her family, she had changed yet again. She wasn't the shy scrub nurse, nor was she the seductive party girl from the night before. At home, she was the eldest daughter, motherly and responsible.

They were a lively group, jammed around the big table that occupied most of the large kitchen. The air hummed with the sound of their collective voices and clinking silverware. They included Bennett in their conversation about the yearly exposition they were attending that day. Mr. Calder and his oldest son, Dylan, had already left to open the booth featuring crafts and food made by the Calder family. The other family members would be departing as soon as breakfast was over. Except for Grandmother Nony, who volunteered to stay behind and keep an eye on Great-Gramma.

He found their acceptance heartening and yet disconcerting. They made him feel like he belonged. But Bennett had no claim to their generosity. His presence was purely accidental. If he hadn't been in Lacy's apartment when the phone call had come, he would not be here.

"So how long have you and Lacy been going out?" asked Mrs. Calder.

"Mother," Lacy said, "Bennett's just a friend."

Yeah, sure. Mrs. Calder's expression was easy to read. She thought they were in a serious relationship.

That's when Bennett knew his suspicions about Lacy were true. She didn't bring strangers home to meet her folks. That's why they accepted him so readily. Her family assumed if he was here, then their relationship was a serious one.

Bennett gulped. What had he gotten himself into? Lacy was a nice girl with traditional values, just as he'd suspected when he'd first laid eyes on her in the operating suite and told himself—*This one is off-limits.*

Seeing Lacy in her home environment told him everything he needed to know. This girl could never be a casual fling. The bold woman he'd met at the nightclub had been a front, a ruse. She'd played a part, pretending to be something she wasn't.

Why?

And yet, those kisses. They'd certainly been real and as hot and passionate as any he'd ever received. They had not been an act.

But he had no space in his life for anything beyond a casual love affair. Pursuing his hard-won career goals prevented him from looking for love.

At least for now.

And he couldn't ask her to wait for him. Lacy was in the prime of her life. Surely, she would want to marry and have children soon. That's what she deserved. She needed a man who had the time to lavish her with attention, not a harried young surgeon scrabbling to build a career and pay off astronomical student loans.

Bennett felt strangely wistful that he wasn't going to be part of this loving family, but he also felt claustrophobic, as if something beyond his control was drawing him into...what? For an educated man, he was having a great deal of difficulty expressing himself.

Then there were those cuff links that were resting in the front pocket of his shirt where Lacy's great grandmother had dropped them when he tried to give the things back to her. The cuff links with the strange symbolism.

Thunderbolt. Love at first sight. Whirlwind courtship. His parents' bad marriage. No thank you.

It wasn't that he didn't care about Lacy. He did. Very much. Probably too much. But he didn't want her expecting something from him that he simply couldn't give. Not at this point in his life. He refused to fall in love or to get married before he was ready.

His parents had made that tactical error, and it had almost ruined them.

Those childhood memories were unpleasant. Spending Christmas holidays with his mother one year, his father the next. Never a real family, always split between two warring factions. He recalled his parents bickering over who was going to pay for his dental work or buy the Little League uniforms. He remembered long lonely nights spent hugging his pillow and wondering how he could make his folks like each other.

Finally, he'd realized he wasn't to blame. What had caused the problem was red hot physical attraction. If his parents had taken their time getting to know each other, they would have realized they were completely incompatible and that a union between them would never have worked out and they could have saved so much agony.

Then again, if they'd done that, Bennett wouldn't be here.

"Grandmother Nony," Lacy said, "if we're stuck here until Dylan can look at my car, you might as well go to the expo with everyone else. Bennett and I can check on Great-Gramma."

"Are you sure?" Grandmother Nony perked up. "I was really hoping my apple preserves might win first prize."

"Go," Bennett said, then realized suddenly that he and Lacy would be alone on the farm except for Great-Gramma tucked away in bed. Was that what he wanted? To be alone with Lacy?

Yes, he decided. They needed to talk and clear the air between them, and he needed to find out if she really believed in this thunderbolt thing her great-grandmother had been talking about. Absentmindedly, he patted the pocket with the cuff links.

A knock sounded at the back door.

Lacy's mother waved at a tall, gangly man standing on the stoop. "Lester, come in."

Work hat in his callused fingers, Lester pushed open the screen door and stepped inside, leaving it slightly ajar behind him.

"I heard about Granny Kahonachek, and I just stopped by to see if she was okay before I headed on over to the expo..." Lester's gaze settled on Lacy, and his words trailed off. "Lacy, you're home."

Bennett didn't like the look in the other man's eyes. Not one bit. It didn't take a rocket scientist, or a heart surgeon for that matter, to figure out the guy had a major crush on her.

Jealousy wrapped around him and squeezed tight.

"Hi, Lester," Lacy said cheerfully, but she didn't meet the man's goo-goo eyes. Obviously, she didn't return his affection.

Bennett felt a spike of triumph, and he had the urge to shout, "Yeah!" Then he immediately wondered why. He had no claim on Lacy Calder. None whatsoever. She was free to date anyone she wanted.

The screen door flapped in the early morning breeze. Lester stayed posed in the doorway, visually gobbling up Lacy.

Bennett imagined plowing a fist in Lester's face for no good reason other than it pleased him and that was scary business.

"Bennett," Lacy's grandmother Nony said, "try some of my red-eye gravy." She hovered at his elbow, gravy boat in hand.

From the corner of his eye, Bennett saw something streak through the back door and into the kitchen. Several people shouted at once, "Lester, get Frank Sinatra out of here!"

Frank Sinatra?

Bennett frowned at the same moment an evil-eyed goat dashed between Grandmother Nony's legs, heading straight for the breakfast table.

Grandmother Nony lost her balance. Her hands flew into the air.

The gravy boat went up.

And then came down.

Smack-dab in Bennett's lap.

❧ 10 ❧

"I'M so SORRY about your pants," Lacy apologized. "And about the clothes dryer being broken."

Bennett glanced at her. Everyone had gone to the farm expo, leaving them alone save for Great-Gramma snoozing upstairs. Lacy was leaning on her crutches, watching him hang his Levi's and white long-sleeved shirt on the clothesline.

Being too tall to borrow a pair of pants from anyone in her family, Bennett wore nothing but boxer shorts, his loafers, and a bathrobe that belonged to Lacy's father belted at his waist.

"No harm done." He smiled at her. "My jeans should be dry by the time we wake up from our nap."

It was after ten o'clock, and the moderate weather of early morning had given way to eighty-five-degree temperatures. As a Bostonian, he wasn't accustomed to such a warm spring climate.

"Come on," Lacy said. "I'll show you to the guest quarters above the barn, but don't expect anything fancy. It's where the extra farmhands stay during harvest."

"Hey, all I need is a place to lay my head. I've slept on exam tables. It can't be any worse than that."

"Follow me." She crooked a finger, then ambled off. She was getting pretty good with those crutches, swinging along at a nice clip.

Unbidden, his eyes traveled from the crutches to Lacy's delectable behind encased so enticingly in that pale floral jumper. He wanted so badly to fill his hands with her lush tush, fill his nose with her scent, fill his eyes with the sight of her set free from her clothes.

He realized suddenly she'd gone off and left him standing with his mouth agape like some love-addled teen. Bennett had to take two long-legged strides to catch up with her.

"What's the deal between you and this Lester character?" he surprised himself by asking.

"Lester's had a crush on me since we were kids." Lacy sighed. "He's asked me to marry him about a hundred times."

"No kidding."

She nodded.

"He's a good-looking guy. Why haven't you ever taken him up on his offer?"

"I don't love him. And sweet as he is, Lester's main interests are cows and corn and not much else." Lacy made a face. "Why do you ask?" She stopped outside the large red barn about a hundred yards from the house and turned to look at him.

"No reason."

"You wouldn't be jealous, would you?" She slanted him a coy glance. She looked so cute in her buttercream jumper with her hair pulled into a ponytail.

"Me? Jealous?"

Jealous as Othello over Desdemona. Jealous as Popeye over Olive Oyl. Jealous as a kid over siblings.

Okay, the last example wasn't so hot. But the thought of Farmer Lester with his dirt-stained paws roving over Lacy's tight little body made Bennett's blood run icy.

"I don't do jealousy," he said.

"What?" She frowned at him.

Bennett shifted. Had he actually said that? What a jerk. "What I mean is, well, jealousy is a destructive emotion born of passion, and I try not to let my emotions get the better of me."

"Oh." She looked damned disappointed while at

the same time so much swirled in her eyes—heat, need, desire.

"I'm trying to explain something to you." He reached out and touched her arm. Despite the words he knew he sounded pompous, and all-too-doctorly. He ached to experience deep passion with her. He wanted to see her wild, out of control, nuts with desire for him.

"Lacy, there's something I have to tell you."

"Yes?"

"It's the reason I don't allow my sexual urges to run my life."

She nodded and her eyes rounded big. "I'm listening."

He let go of her arm, too distracted by the softness of her skin. "My parents met at Cape Cod one weekend, on the beach. Their attraction was instant. Like being hit by a freight train, my mother said. And like a freight train running off the track at high speed, that attraction ruined their lives."

She waited, said nothing.

He took a deep breath, ran his hand through his hair, and continued.

"They made love the very day they met and conceived me. They were both still in college, both studying to be doctors. The last thing they needed was to get married, but that's what they did. Unfortunately, med school and parenthood are demanding propositions on their own. Put the two together, and something's got to give. The powerful passion between my father and my mother turned from love into hate. They fought constantly and divorced when I was two. They still can't stay in the same room together. I vowed I would never make a major life decision based on passion."

He felt her gaze on his face. Unable to meet her eyes for fear of giving away his growing feelings for her, he stared intently at Frank Sinatra, who was blithely munching weeds underneath the clothesline.

Bennett studied the goat, anxious for something to take his mind off his emotional turmoil. One minute he was struggling against the urge to take Lacy into his arms and kiss her. The next minute he was ready to rip his jeans and shirt off the clothesline, wet or not, shimmy into them, and hitchhike back to Houston. Because the longer he lingered here, the more he yearned to stay.

Because no matter how attracted he might be to Lacy, her wacky lovable family, and West, Texas, they had no place in his future.

None at all. Keeping their relationship strictly platonic was in her best interest as well as his.

"Can you get the gate?" she asked softly. "I can't get it open and stay up on the crutches."

"Oh, yeah, sure." Jerking his head from his worrisome thoughts, he hurried ahead to unlatch the gate and usher her through.

"And the barn door." She nodded.

He opened that too,

The barn was airless, musty, and filled with hay and sacks of grain. Dust motes swirled in the dim fight seeping in through the dusty windows.

Lacy sneezed.

"Bless you."

She beamed at him and rested her crutches against the wall. She looked like a teenager, free of makeup, her hair off her face.

"Bed's upstairs." She pointed to the stairway at the back of the barn.

Bennett watched, totally mesmerized by her. He licked his lips. His pulse hammered. His stomach squeezed.

His body ignored all his mind's earlier admonitions.

He wanted her and no amount of logic and common sense could talk him out of it.

Lacy's insides wobbled like a sailboat in a hurricane. It was official. Bennett didn't believe in the thunderbolt.

Question was, did she still believe? Or had she been a romantic fool all these years?

She was having a crisis of faith. First, she'd discovered the thunderbolt wasn't quite as infallible as her great-grandmother had always claimed and now Bennett revealed the depressing story of his parents' experience with their version of the thunderbolt. The last thing she wanted was to hurt him in any way.

She should leave the barn immediately. She'd shown him where his room was. Nothing good could come of staying here with him.

But she couldn't make herself go.

Okay, what if the thunderbolt wasn't real? It didn't alter the fact that she was very attracted to Bennett. She wanted to make love to Bennett whether he was the one or not. Their affair didn't have to end happily ever after.

Sex and love were two different things, and she was fully beginning to realize that. Perhaps what she felt for Bennett was nothing but runaway lust.

If that were true, a lusty roll in the hay would satisfy and they could get on with their separate lives.

For hours she had been unable to think of anything but kissing him again. In the car on the way here, beside him at the breakfast table, upstairs in her great-grandmother's bedroom. Her lips ached for his mouth; her arms yearned to wrap around his neck; her nose itched to bury itself in his chest. She wanted to smell him, touch him, taste him, feel him.

She wasn't pretending to be something she wasn't any longer. Nor was she still tied to some bizarre familial myth. The time had come to free herself. To simply be Lacy, with no agenda or hidden motive other than to be with Bennett.

For once in her life, she felt no embarrassment over her sexuality, no shame at her inexperience.

In her pocket lay the condom CeeCee had given her the night before. She'd forgotten to take it out of her jumper, and now she was glad.

She wanted Bennett, and she didn't care if he loved her or not. Sure, it would be nice if he returned her affections, but she was tired of believing in fairy tales. Tired of waiting for the perfect man. She wanted to know what it was like to be a woman. To have a man desire her, hold her, make love to her. If he walked away from her after they had sex, she would survive.

She angled him a come-hither glance.

And he came hither at blinding speed.

"Be careful." He wrapped an arm around her

waist. "You could fall so easily balancing on one leg like that."

His chest was pressed against her back, his hips flush with hers.

There was no mistaking his arousal.

Lacy turned her head. Her cheek brushed his chin. Their lips were so close.

Then indecision struck, and she began to tremble. Her belief in her plan flew away, and she was left with the stark reality of what she wanted and what was about to happen between them.

Bennett groaned, low and guttural.

The barn smelled earthy, rich, sexy. Thick mounds of coarse hay were strewn across the floor not two feet away. The thought of her bare flesh pressed against that rough hay made her tremble all the harder.

Tremble with starving, desperate need.

She'd waited so long for this.

It was warm in the enclosure. Beads of perspiration formed at the hollow of her throat. She saw that he was sweating, too, droplets glistening on his forehead.

She wanted to lick his skin and taste his salty flavor. She wanted to peel back that bathrobe and get her hands on what lay beneath. She wanted to skyrocket to heaven in his arms.

Oh, the things she wanted!

Lacy's lips parted, but before she could whisper a word, his mouth covered hers in a spectacular kiss.

His hands spanned her waist, holding her steady. His breathing was raspy, ragged. His tongue teased and coaxed. His eyes shone feverish with desire.

Lacy turned into his arms, and he lifted her to his chest. Without uttering a sound, he took her to the hay and arranged her gently on the floor.

He ripped the bathrobe from his body and tossed the garment aside, baring his muscular chest. He stood in nothing but his boxer shorts, and the you're-the-most-sexy-thing-I've-ever-laid-eyes-on expression on his face told her that he wanted exactly the same thing she wanted.

Their bodies joined together. Here. In the barn. On the hay. All emotional consequences be damned.

She spread her knees and reached out her hands to him. He lowered himself between her legs, careful to avoid jostling her injured foot, and gently began to kiss her again.

Finally, at long last, she would know what it was like to be a woman.

And if the thunderbolt was real, then he would be hers forever. If it wasn't real, then at least she'd have this one moment of exquisite pleasure to treasure of her first time with a handsome, virile man.

MAKING LOVE TO LACY SEEMED THE MOST NATURAL thing in the world.

Never mind the annoying voice in the back of his brain telling him that he was getting in over his head. Never mind that his breath quickened with fear half as much as with excitement. Never mind that he was leaving Texas in less than a week.

His hands were unerring. His lips sure. More than anything, he wanted to give and receive pleasure with this woman.

And Lacy seemed as eager as he to consummate their union. The tension that had smoldered between them from the moment he had sauntered into the operating room at Saint Madeleine's burst into a full-fledged forest fire.

She was the picture of his every adolescent fantasy sprung to life and more wonderful than he had ever dreamed. She was lush and fresh and eager. His hands shook with need. His heart pounded with passion.

Her warm, moist lips clung to his tighter than any embrace. Sensuous lips that were an odd combination of wildness and innocence.

What an intriguing paradox she was. Sweet and naughty.

At times she seemed almost virginal, and then in the next moment she would turn into the most tempting of temptresses. His eyes never left hers as his fingers slowly unbuttoned her jumper. She wriggled free from the clothing, and when he saw her body wrapped only in that pink satin teddy, he sucked in his breath with admiration.

"You're so beautiful."

She blushed prettily and ducked her head.

"I mean it."

"I'm not used to hearing men talk to me like this," she said softly.

"Well, you should be. You're a spectacular woman, and any man would be lucky to have you. I'm damned lucky to be here with you right now."

"Really?" She raised her head and blinked at him. The tender expression on her face slugged him in the solar plexus.

"Are you sure this is what you want, Lacy?" he whispered. "You know I can't promise you any more than this moment. I can't promise you tomorrow."

"Tomorrow will take care of itself," she said. "Make love to me, Bennett. I want you; I need you…"

Was it his imagination or did the words "I love you" hang unspoken in the air?

Did she love him?

Bennett pulled back and searched her face, and he

saw something suspect in her eyes. The last thing he wanted was to break her tender heart. He couldn't stand the thought of knowing that he'd hurt her.

"Lacy..."

But before he could question her further, she raised up on her elbows and flicked the tip of her hot pink tongue and licked his nipple.

Bennett inhaled as sharply as if he'd been scalded. Such heat. Such intensity. Such indescribable delight.

Sheer ecstasy.

Moaning softly, he kissed her again, his arms cocooning her.

"Bennett." She murmured his name. "Oh, Bennett."

"I'm here, cupcake, right here."

He lowered his head, then nipped and kissed and tickled her skin with his tongue. He visited her neck, her cheek, her eyelids, her earlobes until she was writhing restlessly beneath him.

"Every time I avoided your eyes in surgery it was because I was secretly longing to do this," he said.

"No kidding?" she breathed.

"From the moment you fell off your stool at my feet."

Her cheeks flushed with embarrassment. "I imagined you thought I was the world's biggest klutz, but the truth is, you unnerved me that much."

"I thought you were adorably disarming." He eased the straps of her teddy over her shoulders, then traced an index finger over her tight breasts.

Mesmerized, he watched as her nipples responded to his touch, growing harder, more prominent with each circling caress. When he dipped his head to suckle there, she arched her back and moaned low in her throat.

He ran his hand downward, skimming first her waist, then her flat, firm belly. She writhed against his hand, whimpered for more.

The woman surprised him at every turn. She gazed at him coyly as if completely unaware of what she did to him. Well, two could play that teasing game.

Inch by inch, his hand delved lower, igniting a blazing path of eager response.

"Oh," she whispered when his fingers curled at her most feminine part. "Oh." She grabbed handfuls of hay and whimpered shamelessly, her back arching off the barn floor.

She was the most desirable woman he had ever known. For this brief moment in time, she belonged to him alone.

"Don't stop," she begged when he moved his hand to gently rub the inside of one thigh as soft and irresistible as heavenly meringue.

"Do you like what I'm doing to you?"

In answer, she fiercely grabbed his hair in both fists and brought his mouth down to hers.

Every muscle in her body tensed as he continued to stroke between her legs. Her flavor filled his mouth in an explosion of epic proportions. Nothing had ever tasted this good. Not the juiciest filet mignon. Not the sweetest birthday cake. Not the finest caviar.

She clung desperately to him, her escalating passion kindling his desire to unbearable heights.

❧ 11 ❧

LACY FELT as if she were walking on a piece of string stretched taut across the Grand Canyon. One infinitesimal slip and she would plunge down, down, down into the beautiful abyss.

She was both scared and awed. Wanting to tumble so badly but frightened of what lay below the myriad sensations assaulting her body at Bennett's every touch.

The power he held in one finger took her breath and her will. She would follow this man anywhere. Thunderbolt or no, he belonged to her, whether he recognized that fact or not. They belonged together. Making love would cinch their connection. After that, could he abandon his destiny?

Then suddenly, without warning, Bennett rolled away from her.

She stared at him. "What's wrong?"

"We...I can't do this."

"Why not?"

"No protection." His voice was a croak. He pulled ragged breaths. "I can't believe I let things go this far."

"Wait." Lacy reached for her jumper, thrown haphazardly to one side in the hay. She dug in the pocket for the condom CeeCee had given her the day before. Silently, she said a prayer of thanks for her friend's foresight.

Had it really been less than twenty-four hours since she'd sashayed into the Recovery Room with the intention of learning how to flirt?

Things were moving too fast, but she knew this was right. She would not regret this, no matter what the outcome might be. Better to have Bennett for a short while than not to have him at all.

"You're prepared?" He looked astonished but took the foil square she extended toward him.

She shrugged.

"Lacy Calder," he murmured, gathering her into his arms once more. "You surprise me at every turn."

"I've got another surprise for you," she confessed.

"Oh?"

She cleared her throat, unsure how to tell him. "I've never really done this before."

"What do you mean?"

"Well...I'm kind of a virgin."

"Excuse me?" He looked incredulous. "Kind of a virgin? How can you be kind of a virgin?"

She shrugged again.

"Really?" He looked gobsmacked.

She nodded, feeling too shy to say much.

He gulped. "But why me? Why now?"

She desperately wanted to tell him that she loved him. That she'd been felled by the legendary thunderbolt, and that's all there was to it, but she knew that would most probably send him sprinting off across Lester's back pasture at a speed to rival a Kentucky Derby winner.

And honestly, she couldn't blame him if he did. The thunderbolt was a rather unbelievable story if you hadn't grown up hearing about it day in and day out. Bennett was a doctor. A man of science. He would no more swallow the thunderbolt myth than he would believe her if she told him she was pregnant was Elvis's love child.

Especially since Lacy was seriously doubting the thunderbolt herself. But she did believe in her feelings. Surely her heart would not lead her astray. So

Lacy said what she had to say to keep him at her side and put that lusty gleam back in his eyes.

"I'm twenty-seven years old, Bennett. I think it's time. I like you, but I'm also realistic. I know you won't be in town much longer, but you make me feel sexy and desirable. I want you to be the one."

"You would give me such a precious gift?" His voice went husky, and she could have sworn his eyes misted. "Especially since you waited for so long?"

"Don't read that much into it," she said, struggling to keep things light. She didn't want to make him feel guilty if he chose to have sex with her and then just leave.

She was an adult. She knew exactly what she was proposing. She realized there was no guarantee, no thunderbolt, no myth. Just a woman making love a man to the best of her abilities.

"Lacy..." He looked uncomfortable. "Are you really sure? You've waited your whole life for this."

"And so far, no Prince Charming on a snow-white stallion." *Until you.* She looked at him and smiled shyly. "Please."

"Cupcake, you are the sexiest woman I've ever met, and right now, I want to make love to you more than anything in the world. But as I told you before, I can't make any promises. For the next several years, my life isn't my own."

"I know," she whispered, and sudden fear swamped her. "I'm not asking for happily ever after."

She studied the firm line of his jaw, saw the tenderness in his eyes, and knew she had to try. Perilous as it seemed, it really would be better to love and lose than never love at all.

And who knew? If there was by some small chance a thunderbolt, maybe having sex would bind him to her in a way nothing else could. It was a gamble, but she was ready to spin the wheel, roll the dice, pull the lever.

Lacy had spent her life hiding in her shyness, too nervous or self-conscious to reach out and grab what she wanted. Was she going to let Bennett walk away simply because she was too afraid to risk getting hurt?

She thought of CeeCee and Janet, and she knew what they would say.

Take a chance.

Lacy took a deep breath and said the bravest thing she'd ever said.

"Make love to me, Bennett. No promises, no strings attached. Let's enjoy what we've got and not worry about tomorrow."

BENNETT CAPITULATED. HOW COULD HE NOT, WITH the sweetest, most honest woman in the world held close in his arms.

Dipping his head, he tasted her lips again, as delicious as Nanna's vanilla custard. Then he slid his mouth lower, to her throat, felt the heat of her pulse jump frantically. The force of his need shook him deeply. He feared his knees would not hold him if he tried to stand.

There was no scrambling away from this. From her. He'd dreamed of this moment since the day he'd met her. Dreamed and tried to tell himself it was an impossible fantasy.

Here she was, offering herself up to him without expectations or demands. She was the most understanding female he'd ever come across, and he treasured each moment with her.

In one expeditious movement, he whisked off his boxer shorts.

Lacy inhaled sharply at the sight of him. Pride filled Bennett, knowing that he had produced such an intense response in her.

He put on the condom, then lay beside her to swirl his fingers at her hot, wet center once more.

"Oh, Bennett."

"Yes, Lacy. Does that feel good?"

"Heaven. I'm in heaven." She clung to his shoulders with both hands. "More. Please, more."

His mouth captured hers. They kissed for one long, earth-shattering moment. Slowly, inch by inch, he slid into her.

When she cried out, he froze, terrified that he might be hurting her, but she shifted beneath him and lifted her hips tentatively.

"I love the way you feel inside me," she gasped. "So strong. So manly."

Her lush naked body was molded by his hands. Those sapphire eyes that had peeped at him so many times over a surgical mask were wide with wonder and desire. He smelled hay and the earthy scent of their combined musk. He was so overcome by sensations that he almost lost control then and there.

"Put your legs over my shoulders. That way there's less of a chance I'll hurt your ankle," he whispered, trying hard to focus on something besides the tremendous fire inside him begging to be released.

This was her first time. He wanted it to be special.

She obeyed, and he ended up with a slim leg resting on each shoulder.

He cupped her face in his hands and carefully began to move again, his eyes never leaving her face as he watched for any signs of discomfort.

A blinding smile raised her lips, revealing to him exactly how much pleasure he was giving her.

"It's fine, Bennett. Truly fine," she said, reading his mind. "It hurt for a second, but now it feels just glorious."

She blinked at him through a fine mist of tears, the smile on her face deepening, and in that moment, Bennett knew he was a goner.

In her eyes, he saw what he feared. Happiness, joy, warmth, and affection. Heat and need and hunger.

And love.

No matter that she would deny it, Lacy Calder loved him.

He should have been terrified. He should have stopped, got up, and walked all the way to Houston. But he didn't want to stop. He didn't want to leave.

In that instant, Bennett had the strangest sensation that he had come home.

His feelings made no sense. He was in a small Texas town, almost two thousand miles from Boston. He was with a woman he'd known barely five weeks. Why he should experience this unwavering sense of belonging, he had no idea.

But he did.

Then Lacy whispered his name, and in the next second a convulsive quiver shook her whole body.

He struggled to hold himself back, fought to hang

on to one shred of control, but it was useless. Inside her, above her, he had no will of his own. Her shudder moved through him, overtook him, and he joined her, burying his face in her neck and gently calling her name.

WHAT HAD THEY DONE?

Bennett woke with a start and stared in confusion at his surroundings.

Then he looked over and saw Lacy nestled in a tight ball against his chest, one fist curled under her chin.

And he panicked.

He had to get out of here.

Gently he eased his arm, which felt no more alive than a wooden stump, out from under her.

She murmured in her sleep, a lock of hair the color of melted sunshine curling across her cheek. He had the strongest urge to brush that curl away, touch that tender cheek. But if he did, he might awaken her, and he wasn't prepared for that.

Before he faced her and told her he was going back to Houston, he wanted to get dressed. A man could make a better case for abandoning the woman he'd just made love to when he was fully clothed.

He found his boxer shorts and borrowed bathrobe —how had his clothes gotten halfway across the barn? —slipped into them and then stumbled outside. He blinked against the brightness of the noonday glare.

His head felt stuffy, his gut empty, and his conscience fired with guilt.

Running out on her, eh, Bennett?

He wasn't a heartless heel. In fact, this was for her own good as much as his. Through his parents he had learned that you couldn't trust emotion, that passion was suspect. The intense feelings he had for Lacy only proved that he must leave her to save them both.

Oh, yeah? Then why did you make love to her even after you found out she was a virgin?

Why? Because he was weak. Because physically, he had wanted Lacy more than he had any other woman.

And because, he admitted to himself, *he* was bailing out before *he* got hurt.

He knew he could not stay in Texas. He had a future in Boston. Obligations there. And he'd promised himself after Nanna's death that he would open up a heart center. He even planned on erecting a clinic on the plot of land in downtown Boston that

Nanna had left him. And he'd promised himself he would never trust love born of intense passion.

A slight breeze kicked up and blew at the tufts of hair on his chest, making Bennett realize he was standing in the barnyard wearing nothing but his undershorts and Lacy's father's bathrobe.

Get your pants on and get out of here. Pronto. Call a taxi, rent a car, hitchhike. Hurry. Before Lacy's family catches you half naked with this guilty look on your face.

Spurred on by that unpleasant thought, he sneaked around the barn, through the gate, and into the backyard. His single goal—his Levi's, hanging on the clothesline.

Except when he got to the clothesline, Bennett was stunned to see Frank Sinatra calmly chewing on his blue jeans. The pesky old goat had already consumed half of one leg.

"You son of a billy goat," Bennett shouted and stalked toward the gluttonous creature. "Get away from my pants!"

The goat stopped in mid-swallow, a hunk of denim dangling from the corner of his mouth. Bennett stormed closer, verbally berating the goat's entire ancestry.

Frank Sinatra's back legs stiffened. His eyes rolled back in his head. Tremors ran through his body, and then, to Bennett's horror, the goat keeled over onto his side and lay immobile.

Bennett ran over and knelt beside the goat who did not appear to be breathing. His shouting had caused the old goat to have a heart attack.

Terrific! He'd killed Great-Gramma Kahonachek's prize possession. He was a goat murderer. A *cabrito* assassin.

Bennett's stomach pitched as he imagined telling Great-Gramma that Frank Sinatra had expired. What if the negative news was too much to take and the elderly lady suffered a heart attack, too?

Lacy would be devastated.

What to do?

He had no choice but to dispose of the carcass.

Bending, he scooped the deceased goat into his arms. Where could he hide the body until he had time to ease Great-Gramma into the notion that she would never see Old Blues Eyes again?

Lugging the heavy animal, he pivoted on one heel. To the right lay the house, to the left the road, behind him the barn.

Think, Sheridan, think.

Goat hair tickled his nostrils.

He sneezed.

Bennett realized he looked totally ridiculous. How had he, a surgical thoracic resident from

Boston, come to find himself nearly naked in the backyard of a Texas farmhouse, a dead goat in his arms, his half-consumed blue jeans lying on the lawn?

It was preposterous. Laughable.

He sneezed again.

Great. Super. Stupendous.

Then he thought of a line from his favorite Mel Brooks movie, *Young Frankenstein*.

Could be worse. Could be raining.

It wasn't raining.

But something else unexpected happened.

The goat stirred.

Bennett was so startled, he stumbled backward into the picnic table.

The goat lifted his head, stared Bennett straight in the eyes, and bleated long and loud.

Bennett yelled.

The goat kicked.

They both fell to the ground in a tangled heap of hands and hooves.

Quickly, Frank Sinatra recovered, springing to his feet and trotting away.

Bennett stared at the sky, feeling like the biggest idiot on the face of the earth.

"Bennett! Are you okay?"

He looked over to see Lacy hobbling toward him,

her eyes wide with concern, her blond hair tumbling about her shoulders.

"I heard you hollering and came running as fast as I could."

He considered the situation and then started to laugh. So much for a clean, painless getaway.

"What's so funny?" Lacy cocked her head quizzically.

Bennett propped himself on his elbows and waved a hand at the goat. "Frank Sinatra was eating my blue jeans. I yelled at him, and he keeled over. I thought I'd killed him. I thought he was dead. I didn't know how to break the news to your grand-mother, so I picked him up to hide the body." He waved at the goat, who was in the corner of the yard giving Bennett the evil eye. "As you can see, he's fine."

Lacy slapped a palm over her mouth. "Oh, Bennett, I'm so sorry. I forgot to tell you that Frank is a Tennessee fainting goat. They pass out when they feel threatened."

"No kidding."

Their eyes met. Lacy dropped her hand and grinned at him.

"You're a city boy through and through."

"Tell me about it," he said, getting to his feet and dusting himself off.

"That was sweet of you to try and protect my grandmother."

"Hey, I didn't want to have to tell her that I'd killed her favorite pet."

Lacy's giggle gave his heart wings. "You poor thing. You must have been terrified when Frank woke up in your arms."

"Shocked is more like it," he said, not willing to admit how much the goat had disconcerted him. He was a doctor. How could he not have noticed the goat wasn't dead?

How? Well, it wasn't as if he'd performed a post-mortem on the darned thing, but mostly it was because his mind had been filled with sensuous thoughts of Lacy. Thoughts that hit him like the A-bomb whenever he dared look at her. Thoughts that could lead them both into serious trouble.

Lacy limped closer and reached up to pluck a piece of straw from his hair. She swayed on her good leg. Bennett put an arm around her waist to brace her.

"Where are your crutches?" he asked, erotic sensations flooding his body at her nearness.

"I was in such a hurry to check on you, I forgot them in the barn."

Her lips were close. Too close. He recalled the flavor of those lips, so recently savored. She had tasted like peaches. Like summer and sunshine. Rich, ripe, expansive. Full of life and energy and love.

He peered into those incredible eyes. She stared at him with such trust, such admiration, Bennett's heart stuttered. His feelings were rushing him down a dangerous path. A path that threatened to ruin all his plans.

But he couldn't seem to help himself. As inexplicably as a child drawn to a magician, he cupped her smooth cheek in his palm.

She smiled at him, her emotions shining clearly in her face—pleasure, joy, happiness.

The panic that had overwhelmed him earlier returned with a vengeance. He was going to have to hurt her. Despite all his precautions, he was going to break her heart.

There was no way they could have a happy ending.

At that moment the cell phone in his bathrobe pocket rang.

❧ 12 ❧

"THAT WAS Dr. Laramie." Bennett disconnected the call and turned to face Lacy, who hovered beside his elbow. "Mr. Marshall is getting his heart transplant. They're flying the organ in from Minnesota as we speak. I've got about three hours to get to Houston and scrub in. Unfortunately, I don't have time to wait for your brother to repair your car. Does West have a ride service?"

She shook her head. "No, but surely I can find someone to drive you to Waco to catch the plane."

"All right." Bennett nodded.

Lacy rested her hands on her hips and eyed him. "Since Frank Sinatra made mincemeat of your blue jeans, you're going to need a new pair of pants. We'll borrow from my brothers. What size do you wear?"

"Thirty-two waist, thirty-six length."

She made a face. "You're taller than anyone in the family. Dylan wears a thirty-two-inch waist, but they'll be short on you."

"Anything will do." His apprehension built. He was anxious to get on his way.

"I'll get your shirt off the clothesline and fetch a pair of Dylan's jeans."

Just then, Grandmother Nony's car turned into the driveway. "Hey, kids," she greeted them as she got out. "I came back for more apple preserves. I sold out already." She stopped chattering and stared at them. "Is something the matter?"

"Bennett needs to get back to Houston right away to assist in an emergency heart transplant. With my car out of commission, we need someone to drive him to the airport in Waco. Can you take him?"

Grandmother Nony bared her teeth and sucked in her breath. "Oh dear. I tried to tell your great-gramma that this was a bad idea."

"What was a bad idea?" Lacy's voice went up a notch. Bennett looked from Lacy to her grandmother and back again.

"Taking the cables off your car battery."

"What!"

"I'm sorry, honey. I didn't know it would cause this kind of trouble. Your great gramma insisted you and Bennett had to stay here until he was struck by the thunderbolt. She asked me to disable your car."

"You disabled my car!"

Grandmother Nony winced and nodded.

"I take it the gravy spill wasn't accidental, either." Lacy looked mad enough to spit bullets.

"Well, Great-Gramma said you were pretty mad at her. She wanted to make sure you didn't get away," Grandmother Nony explained.

"The clothes dryer isn't really broken, either, is it?" Lacy asked.

"No," Grandmother Nony admitted.

Lacy smacked her palm with her forehead. "I don't believe this family."

"What's going on? What does this mean?" Bennett asked. "What am I missing?"

"It means"—Lacy gave her grandmother an icy glance— "that my family has been playing meddlesome matchmakers. You're free to leave, Bennett. All we have to do is reattach the cables to the battery, and you can be on your way."

❦

LACY TOOK A DEEP BREATH IN A VAIN ATTEMPT TO calm herself. She'd known from the minute she'd brought him home that she would have to explain her family and their kooky beliefs toward love, marriage, and happily ever after. She also knew that in all likelihood he would not understand. Would in fact, be disgusted with her.

She stood beside Bennett while he replaced the cables. He looked ridiculous in Dylan's much-too-short blue jeans. If the mood between them had been jovial, she would have joked about his being prepared for a flood.

"Explain this thunderbolt thing to me again." He turned his head and angled her a chiding look. "Help me to understand what would make a sweet little grandmother tear apart your car to keep you home."

"It's the funniest thing," she began, purposely keeping her eyes moving so she wouldn't have to meet his gaze. She stared at the oil stains on the underside of the hood. "You're going to laugh, it's so silly."

Bennett straightened, put down the wrench, and wiped his hands on a rag. "That's great. I could use a good laugh."

Her palms were sweaty. Her heart raced. "Well, uh, it's like this."

"Yes?" he prompted.

Lacy studied her feet.

Bennett reached out a hand, cupped her chin in

his palm, and forced her to look at him. His eyes drilled a hole straight through her. "Talk."

Lacy tried to stall. She hemmed and hawed, but Bennett was having none of her diversionary tactics.

"Stop beating around the bush and talk to me. I don't bite."

No, but you'll take a powder.

Lacy sighed. Patience and tolerance were reflected at her from the depth of Bennett's chocolate-brown eyes. There was nothing left to do but tell him the truth and hope against hope that he didn't find her strange or manipulative or foolhardy.

"It's kinda hard to explain."

"You're a bright, articulate woman." He wrapped a hand around her upper arm. "Give it a shot."

"Do you believe in predestination?" Her voice rose on a hopeful note.

"Do you mean do I believe in the concept that we have no free will? That our destinies are mapped out for us even before our births?"

"Well, yeah."

"No. Absolutely not." He shook his head.

"You don't think it's at least possible that you were put here on earth to be a doctor and that even if your life had turned out differently you would eventually find your way to being a physician?"

"I'm not following you."

Lacy wet her lips. "Do you believe in predestined love? That there is one right person for everyone, and when you find that person, you'll know who they are, and they'll know who you are without any doubts?"

"One right person in a planet that houses almost eight billion people? Come on, Lacy, that's a bit far-fetched, don't you think?"

"No," she whispered. "I don't."

"What are you trying to say?"

"I've deceived you, Bennett. I led you to believe that I wanted nothing more than to have a fling with you, but that's not true. My family believes in the power of the thunderbolt and I was raised to believe it too."

Then, in excruciating detail, she told him all about the family thunderbolt legend and how Great-Gramma had fabricated her chest pains in order to get Bennett to bring her to West.

She sneaked peeks at him as she spoke and watched the emotions flit across his face—confusion, irritation, disbelief, and finally disappointment.

"I can't believe your family manipulated me into coming here," Bennett said. "If I didn't know better, I'd say *you* even orchestrated that sprained ankle."

"It's not like that. I had no idea what Great-Gramma was cooking up until we got here."

"But you didn't bother to tell me the truth once you did discover that she was playing matchmaker."

Lacy couldn't look him in the eye. "That's right."

"Why not?" He folded his arms across his chest.

"Because I *did* believe in predestined love. From the minute you popped into the operating suite, I thought you were the man I'd been waiting a lifetime for. Call me a fool, but I know you feel something for me, too, Bennett, but I also know your career is important to you. I foolishly believed that if I gave the thunderbolt some time, then you would realize I'm the one you're supposed to be with. But I was wrong. The thunderbolt is nothing but a stupid legend. You can't force someone to love you."

The silence lengthened between them.

Trembling from head to toe, Lacy raised her chin and met his calm, unreadable gaze.

"Today, I allowed myself to be swept away by my passion for you. And make no mistake, it *is* a powerful attraction. But that's what frightens me. Something that flames this hot is bound to bum out. I will not commit the same mistake my parents made. I'm so sorry if I've hurt you in any way. You're a truly wonderful person, and I know that someday you'll find this thunderbolt you're looking for. But it simply isn't me."

Lacy bit her bottom lip and blinked furiously to keep the tears from spilling down her cheeks.

Janet was right. Love at first sight was nothing but a Cinderella fairy tale. Her mother, grandmother, and great-grandmother had simply been lucky in love, and in turn, they had dubbed that luck the thunderbolt.

But honestly, it was delusional.

For too many years, she had listened to their useless advice. Listened and dreamed dreams she had no business dreaming. She'd envisioned a fantasy man who could not, did not, exist.

"Lacy," Bennett repeated. "I am sorry. If I'd known... If you'd only told me you really believed in this thunderbolt thing, I would never have had sex with you. I know it's going to be hard..."

Lacy raised a hand. "Don't. Please, just don't. Okay? I'll be all right."

She had taken a chance. It hadn't worked out. So there was no such thing as the thunderbolt, after all. She would survive. She was stronger than she suspected. One good thing had come out of this. She'd gotten over her shyness. She'd even made love with a man she loved, even if he didn't love her back.

At the memory of their tender lovemaking, her stomach roiled. Oh, God, she loved him so very much.

"Cupcake," he whispered.

"It's okay."

He placed a hand on her shoulder, but Lacy shrugged him off. "Let's talk about this some more," he said. "I can't promise you anything, but I *do* care about you. We had a great time. Maybe, someday, when I've finished my residency and opened my practice, we could see how we feel then and..."

She whirled on him, sudden anger blooming inside her. She would not be ashamed of or embarrassed by her feelings. She'd made a gigantic blooper in loving him, but she couldn't regret having taken a chance.

She'd learned a lot and she decided that she wasn't going to spend the rest of her life hiding under a rock, waiting for Prince Charming to come kick it over. She was tired of playing Sleeping Beauty. Yes, her lesson was a painful one, but she'd learned it well.

"No, Bennett. If you don't love me now, then you'll never feel it. I can accept that." She pivoted on her good heel, then hurried to the house as fast as she could hobble.

Bennett sat in the commuter airplane, wearing the ridiculous high-water blue jeans that belonged to Lacy's brother, wishing with all his heart that things could have been different between them.

Lacy was so sweet, so lovable. He hated to think he'd hurt her. Damn. It was the last thing on earth he wanted.

He should have known better. He should have realized she was in love with him. He should never have kissed her that first time at the nightclub.

What he hadn't expected was this hollow, aching sensation in the region of his heart. Had he fallen in love with her, too?

But how could he be in love with her? He barely knew her. Sure, they'd worked side by side for hours a day for the last five weeks. Worked in tandem like a well-trained team of trick ponies. Sure, she was one of the cutest, sweetest women he'd ever known. Sure, she aroused him to heights he'd never before experienced. Sure, whenever he caught sight of her, his stomach contracted, and his heart flipped.

But that wasn't love.

What he felt for Lacy was simply animal attraction. Love took time.

A lot of time.

There was no such thing as predestined love. It was a precariously romantic concept that led people to do very dumb things.

But still, it hurt to know that he was the cause of

Lacy's pain. It was all his fault. He should never have allowed things to go this far.

He liked so many things about her. She was good-hearted, warm, and generous. Her playfulness lightened his seriousness. Before he even knew what was going on inside himself, Lacy perceived his feelings, his insecurities. His best qualities emerged whenever he was around her.

He loved the way her voice resonated in his head, so soft and modulated. It was the kind of voice a man could hear for a thousand years and never grow tired of. He adored her aroma of roses and soap. A cozy scent that could revive a man's heart no matter how often he smelled it. He cherished the sugary taste of her lips that reminded him of home-cooked meals and cold winter nights spent curled by the fire.

How could anyone not ache to spend a lifetime tasting such lips? Any man would be lucky to have her.

But he wasn't the man for her. No matter what she might believe about thunderbolts and soul mates and love at first sight. He didn't buy into any of that.

Relationships were built over a long period of time. They were based on honesty, communication, and friendship, not hot passion, intense hormonal rushes, or wayward emotions. Fireworks worked fine for great sex but made for lousy long-term unions.

Besides, how could anything so effortless as his feelings for Lacy be trusted? Yes, they got along like hot chocolate and marshmallows, but that very fact gave him pause. He'd spent his life struggling to become a doctor. It took hard work, long hours, and a lot of money. He appreciated the fact that nothing worth having came easily, and that included falling in love.

Bennett stared glumly at the clouds. Breaking things off with Lacy was the right thing to do.

In fact, he needed to take it one step further. He had to put as much distance between them as possible before his pheromones got the better of him again. He needed to leave Texas for good. After the transplant surgery, he was going to tell Dr. Laramie he wanted to cut his study fellowship short by a week.

With any luck, by this time tomorrow he'd be on his way home to Boston.

❧ 13 ❧

"I T'S OVER between us." Lacy lay across her bed in her apartment, sobbing into her hands. CeeCee and Janet sat on either side of her.

Dylan had driven her from West in her car two days after Bennett had departed. She'd been unable to tell her family that the thunderbolt had failed.

"What do you mean, it's over?" CeeCee asked. "When two people love each other there's always hope."

Fat chance for that. Damn CeeCee and her eternal optimism. "Bennett doesn't love me," she countered.

"How can you be so sure?"

"I found out from Pam that Bennett went back to Boston on the first plane out of George Bush on Monday morning."

CeeCee's mouth dropped. "He ran away?"

"Fast as a scalded dog." Lacy echoed one of Great-Gramma's sayings, then she burst into fresh tears.

"There, there," Janet soothed, gently patting Lacy on the shoulder. "All men are scum."

"No." Lacy wiped her eyes with the back of her hand. "Bennett's not scum. This was my fault." She told her friends about the thunderbolt. "I never told him about the thunderbolt or about Great-Gramma faking her illness until it was too late. Who can blame him for feeling duped?"

"I can blame him," CeeCee said. "He hurt my friend. If he were here right now, I'd kick him in the fanny and ask him what on earth he was doing dumping the best thing that ever happened to him."

"Thanks for your support." Lacy sat up, took the tissue CeeCee offered her, and delicately blew her nose. "But really, this is my responsibility. I'm the one who bought into that thunderbolt nonsense. You'd think I would have stopped believing in fairy tales a long time ago."

"It's hard to fight a family legend," Janet sympathized.

"I can't believe I wasted so many years waiting for the thunderbolt to strike." Lacy shook her head. "I was a fool. I should have been dating and having fun. I should have bought a house and planted a garden. I don't need some mythical knight in shining armor to change my life."

"You go, girl," CeeCee sang.

"I took a gamble. You've got to give me credit for that. For once I went after what I wanted. So what if it blew up in my face?" Lacy spoke firmly, trying to convince herself as much as her friends that she was going to be all right.

But the hole in her soul whispered that she was kidding herself. Yes, she had learned a lot, and yes, she would survive, but without her other half, would she ever be completely whole?

For so long she'd waited for the thunderbolt. Now that it had struck and left her charred to a crisp, she didn't know how to proceed. For twenty-seven years she'd believed that true love would solve everything. She had to face reality.

Bennett didn't want her and honestly, she couldn't blame him.

"How are you this morning, Mr. Osborn?" Bennett consulted the chart in his hand, then glanced at the spry octogenarian sitting up in the hospital bed at Boston General. His wife sat in a chair beside him, their hands clasped together.

Will I ever have that kind of closeness with anyone? Bennett wondered, then immediately thought of Lacy.

It seemed he couldn't stop thinking about her no matter how hard he tried. He'd had such intimacy for the briefest of moments, and his feelings had scared him so much that he had chickened out.

The elderly man laid his free hand over his chest and smiled. "Thanks for fixin' my ticker, Doc." Henry Osborn was a native Texan, and his friendly drawl reminded Bennett too much of where he'd just been. Why did fate seem to keep reminding him of what he'd left behind?

"I've had sixty years with my darlin' bride here, and to tell you the truth, it's not near long enough," Henry Osborn continued.

"I bet you two had a long courtship before you got married"—Bennett nodded— "for your relationship to still be so strong after all these years."

Mrs. Osborn giggled like a schoolgirl and peered at her husband with adoring eyes. "Oh, no," she said. "We had a whirlwind courtship. Henry had come to Boston on business, and we both attended a company party. Our gazes met across a crowded room, and in that instant we both just knew."

Henry nodded and his eyes misted. "I remember

like it was yesterday. I walked right up to her and said, 'You're the gal I aim to marry.'"

Bennett's chest tightened. "Really?"

"We were married three weeks later. When it's right, it's right, young man."

"But how did you know for sure?" His mind whirled with thoughts of Lacy, her wacky family, and the legendary thunderbolt.

Then he thought of his parents. Two sides of the coin. The pros and cons of love at first sight. What made the Osborns different than his parents? Why did one marriage work and the other disintegrate?

Henry touched the left side of his chest again. "You'll know deep down in here, son. All you've got to do is follow your heart. It will never lead you astray."

Bennett moistened his lips with his tongue. "But how do you keep it going? What happens when things get rough? What keeps you from giving up?"

Mrs. Osborn smiled. "Oh, that one is easy, young man. You remember everything you love about the other person, and you never let anything get in the way of that love. Not your job or your in-laws or money problems. You put the other person first. Their needs. Their wants. Their desires. Not yours. Love isn't selfish, young man. If you take care of her and she takes care of you, then I promise, everything will work out fine."

It sounded so wonderful. How he wanted to believe it.

Could Mrs. Osborn be right? He thought of his parents and how they'd put their own needs above each other. Single-minded selfishness had ruined their marriage, not passion. Not love at first sight.

He reached a hand into his pocket and fingered the thunderbolt cuff links he'd been carrying around ever since Lacy's great gramma had given them to him.

Bennett drew in a deep breath as his fingers contacted the warm metal. He held them in his palm, the gold winking in the light from the window.

And then it happened.

He felt something.

Like a zap of lightning zinging through his whole body from his head to his toes, raising the hairs on his arms. In that moment he knew.

He'd been struck by the thunderbolt. Not here. Not now. But eight weeks ago, in a hospital in Houston. And he'd been doing his best to suppress it ever since. Fear had hampered him from speaking his mind. Fear had kept him from admitting the truth to himself.

His heart throbbed. His body tingled. His soul ached to be fulfilled.

He was in love with Lacy Calder.

And there was no doubt about it.

THREE WEEKS AFTER BENNETT LEFT TEXAS, LACY was spreading autoclaved instruments across the sterile field when she glanced up and saw him standing in the doorway. He wore green scrubs, a matching scrub cap, blue shoe covers, and a mask.

Bennett?

She blinked. *Nah.*

Surely this must be a mirage. Bennett was far away in Boston, doing an important service, saving people's lives. She'd been seeing his face an awful lot in her imagination. Maybe she wasn't at work at all, but at home in her bed, dreaming a dream that was going to make her cry when she awoke and found it all a fantasy. She bit her bottom lip to see if she was indeed awake.

Ouch.

Okay, that was painful. Not dreaming, then. She was wide awake.

His eyes drilled into hers like laser beams melting

metal. That crazy, illogical feeling leaped inside her. The thunderbolt. Striking again.

How could it be?

If she wasn't asleep, then she must be having a doozy of a hallucination.

"Lacy," he said, his voice strangely heavy.

Auditory hallucinations. That was bad, wasn't it?

She shook her head and returned her attention to the sterile field, determined to ignore this very realistic figment of her overactive imagination.

His shoe covers whispered against the floor. He was coming closer.

Dear heavens. Her heart scampered into her throat. Her hand, wrapped around a retractor, began to tremble.

"Lacy," he said again. This time he was standing right behind her. "Look at me."

She turned on her step stool. Her ankle, healing but still weak, started to give way beneath her.

"Oh." She dropped the retractor and struggled to regain her balance.

But she didn't have anything to worry about. Bennett was there. His arms were around her.

She looked at him. Time hung suspended.

"Is it really you?" she murmured.

"It's really me." He righted her on the stool but

kept his hands spanned around her waist. They stood eye to eye.

"What are you doing here?" she asked.

"I work here."

"Since when?" She sucked in her breath and got a mouthful of mask.

"I transferred from Boston General. I'm going to finish my residency at Saint Madeleine's under Dr. Laramie."

"But how?" She scarcely dared believe that this was true. "And why?"

"How?" He reached behind him and untied the top string of his mask, so it fell around his neck. "Dr. Laramie agreed to sponsor me."

"You've just broken scrub," she whispered.

"I know."

"You'll have to scrub in again."

"No." He lifted a hand to undo her scrub mask as well, his arm brushing against her cheek in the process. "We'll have to scrub in again."

"Why did you do that?"

"To show you the reason I came back."

She frowned. "I don't get it."

"Do you get this?" He hauled her against his chest and kissed her with a passion that made her pant.

"Oh, Bennett," she murmured.

"Hey, you two! Stop that and get scrubbed in

again. Plus, you've contaminated your sterile field, Lacy," Pam barked from the doorway. She clapped her hands. "Come on, we don't have all day."

Bennett took Lacy's hand and led her from the surgical suite to the scrub sinks.

"What's happened?" she asked him.

"I do love you, Lacy. I was just too scared to admit it. I didn't want to repeat my parents' mistake."

"What made you change your mind?" Her eyes searched his face. She wanted so much to believe him.

"I didn't want to live the rest of my life regretting not having taken a chance on us. You're the best thing that ever happened to me, Lacy Calder."

"Oh, Bennett."

"And I'm sorry if I've caused you one moment of pain. All these years I thought love was about passion and that passion eventually cooled and left you nothing but hurt. But I was wrong, Lacy, so wrong."

"How were you wrong?"

"I now understand that love is about sacrificing your own selfish desires for the good of another. I learned that if I want to have love, I must first give it. Lacy, I want to spend my life pleasing you. Loving you."

She reached up and traced his lips with her

fingers. "I want to please you too. Love you. That's how it should be."

He hitched in a breath and paused for a long moment. "You showed me love was about sharing, caring, and accepting. It might be rough on us for the first couple of years until I finish my residency and get my practice started, but we'll work it out."

"Do you really mean it?" She trembled all over. Did she dare hope? "You're not afraid our relationship will end up like your parents?'"

"I finally realized something. I'm not my father, and you're not my mother. My parents both have the same tempestuous personality. Both are pretty selfish. Neither of us are like that. We're good together. And there's no rush. No hurry. We don't have to get married as my parents did. When we get married, it'll be because we're ready."

"Are you certain?"

"Absolutely."

"I knew you were the one." She grinned.

"And I knew it was you from the beginning. I'm just a slow learner."

"Great-Gramma says the thunderbolt is never wrong and that it can't be denied."

"Great-Gramma is very wise."

"She's going to be so happy."

"Not a quarter as happy as I am. Will you marry

me, Lacy? For better or worse, I never want to be without you again."

Lacy beamed at him, her heart filled to bursting. "As if I could say no."

He bent to kiss her again.

Endorphins collided with adrenaline. Testosterone jumped like the lords of the dance in his lower abdomen. Sheer joy sprinted through his nerve endings.

He drew her closer to him, tasting every delicious inch of her lips. He knew without a hint of doubt that she was meant to be his, forever and always.

The thunderbolt had struck again. Claiming two more hearts, melding them together for all time.

EPILOGUE

THE PREACHER STOOD at the front of the elaborately constructed altar erected in the Calders' backyard. Bible in hand, he gave the crowd a welcoming smile.

"Friends and neighbors," the preacher began. "We are gathered here today to unite this man and this woman in holy matrimony."

Lacy peeked at Bennett. He winked at her. She smiled shyly into the pink roses and baby's breath bouquet clutched in her hand.

"Do you, Kermit Kahonachek, renewing your vows with your bride of seventy-five years, take this woman, Katrina Kahonachek, to be your lawfully wedded wife?"

"I do!" Lacy's great-grandfather's voice rang out

loud and clear as he gazed at the woman who'd been his lifelong soul mate.

"And do you, Katrina, take this man, Kermit, to be your lawfully wedded husband, until death do you part?"

Great-Gramma reached over and took her husband's hand. "You bet I do. I'm not going another seventy-five years without him in my life."

"Then I now pronounce your vows renewed. Kermit, you may kiss your bride."

Lacy's heart swelled with emotion as she watched her great-grandfather draw her great-grandmother to him and kiss her soundly on the lips. Pride, joy, happiness, and hope pressed against her chest.

A cheer went up from the crowd.

Lacy gazed at Bennett to find his eyes fixed on her face. Eyes brimming with love. Her breath ceased in that fine moment. She saw them together many years down the road with their own family clustered around them as they celebrated their own seventieth anniversary by renewing their wedding vows.

"I'm ready to throw the bouquet," Great-Gramma announced several minutes later. "All you single ladies gather around." She winked at Lacy and nodded.

Lacy's unmarried cousins and sisters assembled in a clump along with CeeCee and Janet. They all grinned and waved.

Great-Gramma turned her back to the crowd and launched the bouquet over her head.

It spiraled into the air.

A dozen pairs of arms reached upward, scrambling for the prize. Despite being disadvantaged by her small stature, Lacy was determined to grab that bouquet. She leaped up.

Gotta catch it, gotta catch it.

If anything, the thunderbolt had taught her a valuable lesson. Never take tradition lightly. Come hell or high water, she and Bennett were going to be the next ones married in this clan.

Then, from the corner of her eye, she saw a streak of white. Someone or something moving faster than greased lightning dashed forward.

And snatched the bouquet.

With a bleat of triumph, Frank Sinatra trotted away, the bouquet firmly between his teeth.

The crowd roared with laughter.

"Hey!" Lacy shouted. "You come back here! That's my bouquet, you ornery critter."

Old Blue Eyes trotted faster, ribbon streams breaking loose from the bouquet and flying behind him.

"Faint, you son of a billy goat." Lacy fisted her taffeta bridesmaid gown in her hand to keep from tripping over the long skirt and launched herself after him.

"Hang on, there." Bennett took her elbow as she passed him.

"Let go. I'm getting that bouquet one way or the other."

He peered at her, laughter illuminating his face. "You don't need the bouquet, Lacy. Let Frank Sinatra have his lunch."

"But I want to be the next one married," she insisted.

"You will be."

She blinked at him. "Is this a commitment to a wedding date?"

"Yes, ma'am."

"Oh?" She melted against him and placed a hand on his chest. "Do tell."

"A year from today. Same time, same place, same guest list, with a few additions."

"Like your parents?"

"Yes."

"Will you be ready? Are you sure?"

"Cupcake, I've been struck by the thunderbolt. As you well know, there's no denying it. My residency will be finished. We can start looking for a place to set up my clinic. However, I do have one requirement."

"And what is that?" Lacy asked, gazing into the eyes of her intended.

"Frank Sinatra is to be banned from our wedding."

"Or served up as *cabrito* pate."

"Either, or." His grin widened. "Have I ever told you how beautiful you are?"

"Not in the last five minutes."

"Or how much I love you?"

"Hmm, you might have mentioned it."

"Well, it's time to make sure you thoroughly understand." He squeezed her tighter, and his eyes misted with unshed tears of joy. "Without you, Lacy Calder, nothing in my life has meaning. You're the whipped cream on my strawberry shortcake; you're the morning star in my sky; you're the tomato plants on my balcony."

"No kidding?"

He turned his face to the sky, then grinned and shouted. "Hear me world, I love Lacy."

Her pulse slipped through her veins. Everything she'd ever dreamed of had come true. She'd found her soul mate.

Only one more thing would make her world complete, and that would be for CeeCee and Janet to find the same kind of love she'd found in Bennett's arms. She sent a silent prayer to the heavens, beseeching the thunderbolt to strike in their lives.

But in the meantime, she had her own romance to kindle. Standing on tiptoes, she whispered in his ear.

"Last one to the hayloft is a rotten egg."

<hr/>

DEAR READER,

Readers are an author's life blood and the stories couldn't happen without *you*. Thank you so much for reading. I do appreciate more than you could ever know!

As a nurse for twenty-two years, I brought my medical knowledge to this series and it was such fun using my background in the telling of these stories.

If you enjoyed *The Thunderbolt*, I would so appreciate a review. You have no idea how much it means to authors.

You can check out all the books in the Heartthrob Hospital series here.

Don't miss the second book in the series, The Jinx, where CeeCee falls in love with her best friend.

If you'd like to keep up with my latest releases, you can sign up for my newsletter @ https://loriwilde.com/subscribe/

To check out my other books, you can visit me on the web @ www.loriwilde.com.

Much love and light!
—Lori

EXCERPT FROM THE JINX

CeeCee Adams was cursed.

Hexed.

Jinxed.

Doomed.

Forever unlucky in love and destined to traipse the earth as a single woman, compliments of the Jessup family whammy.

How else to explain the numerous failed marriages and hapless love affairs among the women in her family? And how else could she account for the likes of Lars Vandergrin, a six-foot-four Neanderthal who wrestled for the WWF?

Lars had a grin to melt snow off mountain peaks, sheer blond hair cascading to his waist and hands as grabby as quadruplet two-year-olds at a shopping mall. The man also possessed the same rudimentary disregard for the word "no" as the aforementioned toddlers. For the last three hours she'd fended off his advances while sitting through the latest action-adventure flick and she was quickly running out of patience.

Thanks a million, Grandma Addie. As if dating in this new millennium wasn't difficult enough.

Fifty years ago, her maternal grandmother, Addie Jessup had stolen a gypsy woman's lover. The gypsy, a rather vengeful sort it seems, not only zapped Addie with the evil eye, but damned every Jessup female for three generations. No woman in Addie's direct lineage stayed married. Divorce was as commonplace as swapping cars.

Which was the very reason she never dated any guy for too long. She refused to fall into the same trap as her mother, aunts and older sister, Geena. No multiple marriages for her! No revolving charge account at Neiman-Marcus's bridal registry. No ugly child custody battles.

No siree. She was forever a free spirit. Single and loving it.

Except for times like these.

She had met Lars when he had sought treatment in her physical therapy department for a tom rotator cuff. Over the past three weeks he had pestered her to go out with him. She had finally agreed, hoping to persuade him to appear in the wrestling regalia he wore as the Missing Link for St. Madeleine Hospital's charity bachelor auction held annually the third Friday in July. The auction raised healthcare funds for Houston's inner-city kids.

At the moment they were standing beneath the porch lamp on the front stoop of her apartment. Lars had her pinned against the door, his hot breath fanning the hairs along her forehead, fingers thick as kielbasa twisting the top button of her blouse. She cared deeply about the charity auction but not deeply enough to grant this slab of marble carte blanche access to her body.

"Stop it." She swatted his hand and her charm bracelet jangled. "I don't appreciate being pawed."

"Come on *bay-bee,* you owe me." He puckered his lips.

"Owe you? How do you figure?"

"Shrimp dinner, movie, popcorn."

"Hang on, I'll give you the cash."

"No cash." He shook his head and his hair swung like the artificial blond mane on the My Little Pony her first stepfather had given her for her seventh birthday. "The Missing Link wants kissy-kissy."

"If you don't remove your hands from my body this instant, you'll be singing the John Wayne Bobbitt blues."

He giggled and ground his hips against her. "You're feisty. Lars like that."

"You haven't seen feisty, buster. Hands off." She didn't intimidate easily, but a small splash of fear rippled through her. Lars was a very large man.

Immediately she thought of her good friend and next door neighbor, Dr. Jack Travis. Was Jack home?

She dodged Lars's attempt to kiss her, and shot a glance through the sweltering June darkness to the ground floor apartment across the courtyard. Light slanted through the blinds.

At that moment she would have given anything to be with good old dependable Jack, listening to jazz music, sharing a laugh. Jack had such a great laugh. A resonant sound that made her feel safe, secure and cared for. She valued their platonic relationship far more than he would ever know.

If things got really nasty, she would scream for Jack, but she wouldn't call unless she had no choice. She proudly fought her own battles. Besides, thanks to the curse, she'd had more than her share of run-ins with guys like Lars. Still, it was nice knowing she had Jack as backup.

"Come on, *bay-bee*." Lars cupped his palm against her nape. "Let's go inside."

Over my dead body!

"Listen here, Vandergrin." She splayed a palm

across his chest and cocked her knee, ready to use it if necessary. "Things are moving too fast between us."

"You want me in your bachelor auction? I do a favor for you. You do a favor for me."

Blackmailer.

This time she wasn't quick enough. Lars captured her mouth and gave her a hard, insistent kiss. She was in trouble deep. Forget subtlety. No more Ms. Nice Girl. As for the charity auction, she'd just have to find another celebrity.

"Shove off!" CeeCee jerked her mouth away at the same moment Lars thrust out his tongue. Her forehead accidentally whacked into his chin.

"Yeow" he screamed, and pressed a hand to his mouth. "You made me bwite my tonwue!"

ABOUT THE AUTHOR

Lori Wilde is the New York Times, USA Today and Publishers' Weekly bestselling author of 91 works of romantic fiction. She's a three time Romance Writers' of America RITA finalist and has four times been nominated for Romantic Times Readers' Choice Award. She has won numerous other awards as well.

Her books have been translated into 26 languages, with more than four million copies of her books sold worldwide.

Her breakout novel, *The First Love Cookie Club*, has been optioned for a TV movie as has her *Wedding Veil Wishes* series.

Lori is a registered nurse with a BSN from Texas Christian University. She holds a certificate in forensics, and is also a certified yoga instructor.

A fifth generation Texan, Lori lives with her husband, Bill, in the Cutting Horse Capital of the World; where they run Epiphany Orchards, a writing/creativity retreat for the care and enrichment of the artistic soul.

Clay

Jonah

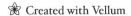

Made in United States
North Haven, CT
08 April 2023

35190438R00139